SCHOOLED

CODENAME: WINGER #2

JEFF ADAMS

BIG GAY
Media

SCHOOLED

CODENAME: WINGER #2

JEFF ADAMS

ISBN: 978-1-7355680-0-3

PRAISE FOR
CODENΔME: WINGER

"A fun and intriguing adventure with fast-paced action and a delightfully authentic voice in Theo. Part mystery, part thriller, and all heart."

TJ KLUNE, NEW YORK TIMES
BESTSELLING AUTHOR OF *THE
EXTRAORDINARIES*

"An unforgettable thrill ride! Equal parts smart and suspenseful."

JULIAN WINTERS, AWARD-WINNING
AUTHOR OF *RUNNING WITH LIONS*

"Theo is a sixteen-year-old junior in high school, a tech whiz, and a swoonable cocktail of sweet and tough. He's exactly the kind of character I want to read about."

GREGORY ASHE, AUTHOR OF THE
HOLLOW FOLK SERIES

ONE

THE BELL RINGING for lunch was the best sound ever. My stomach grumbled as I put my economics book and tablet into my backpack and headed for the door. It took a lot of restraint not to push my way through my classmates who were way too slow.

It sounded like there was a monster in my belly. Coach had put the team on a new training regimen when we returned from holiday break two weeks ago. He designed it to improve our stamina for the second half of the hockey season. The side effects were muscle pain, occasional leg cramps if I didn't cool down properly, and an appetite that turned me into a ravenous beast.

In the hall, I moved quickly, weaving around my classmates like I was avoiding defensemen on the ice.

Eddie was right on time, as always, at the intersection of the science and English wings. He shouldered his messenger bag, fell in step next to me, and interlocked his fingers with mine.

"How's my favorite hockey player?" We slowed down just enough for him to kiss me on the cheek. With the swim season under way, he looked forward to lunch as much as I did.

"I'm good now that I'm with my favorite swimmer." I gave his hand an extra squeeze.

"Theo Reese," Mrs. Hollingsworth called from behind. "A moment, please?"

This was not a good time to consult with the computer-science teacher. I'd been in her advanced class for three days when I was a freshman, and we had quickly determined that I already knew her curriculum. We became friends, though, and we often chatted about technology. I enjoyed her spin on the latest and admired that she kept up, even though she taught pretty basic stuff to most of her students.

"Doesn't she know it's lunchtime?" Eddie asked.

"How often do teachers care about that?" I didn't let Eddie go, and we cut across the crowd to get to her. "Hey, Mrs. H," I said when we got to her classroom doorway.

"I know you're on your way to lunch, and I promise I won't keep you long. I wanted to float something by you." She turned from me to Eddie. "Could we speak alone?"

"Go on. I'll catch up to you." I let Eddie's hand go. "Can you get me a chicken sandwich?"

"Sure can. Try not to get lost in a lot of tech talk." He grinned at me. He wasn't wrong; this kind of discussion was my weakness.

He raised his cute eyebrows at me before he dashed off to join the lunch line.

Mrs. H stepped into her room and I followed. "The computer-science club has a competition in two weeks and it involves cyber security. Each team comes to the competition with a file that contains a secure document. In turn, the other teams have to try and crack the encryption. I know security is a specialty of yours, and I wondered if I could persuade you to come in and look at our work, offer advice —" She hesitated for a moment and that was weird. "—and travel with the team to consult on-site."

Wow. This was completely unexpected. I knew the club worked on some advanced projects and competed occasionally, but I didn't know they got into stuff like this. I didn't expect to be invited to participate, and I suspected I could crack their projects in my sleep.

"Doesn't the club usually meet when I'm off campus?" The proposal intrigued me, but I enjoyed afternoons at MIT where I took classes that challenged me. "I'm not sure I could swing that since the semester's just started."

She looked sheepishly at the floor. "I might have gotten clearance from Dr. Shorofsky. He said he'd consider it to be credit toward your lab assignments since it's only a couple of weeks."

"Um. Okay." I didn't know quite what to say. "How'd you even know who to ask?"

"I've got connections." Based on the devious look in her eye, I decided not to ask more. I had my ways to get information and I shouldn't be surprised she did too.

"I can work with the team on what they've developed and point them in the right direction to increase the security. I wouldn't feel right consulting on-site. I'd be a...."

"A ringer, to borrow one of your sports metaphors. Yes, you probably would be." She guided me farther into the classroom. "There's a quarter-million-dollar prize for this competition—half goes to the school, a quarter goes to the club, and the rest splits up among the students to use for college. It will be cutthroat among the teams. Imagine what this program could become with that money, not to mention the cash the individuals would have for their college funds.

The team is doing good work, and I'm not asking you to do any for them. Like you suggested—hack what they create and guide them to make it better. During the competition, you could make sure they're going in the right direction."

"Ah, Mr. Reese, there you are," Coach Daly said.

Why was everyone calling me from behind today? I wanted some lunch and time with my man. But for Coach to look for me now—that wasn't a good sign.

"Mrs. Hollingsworth, do you mind if I borrow him?"

The plea in her eyes surprised me. This was super important to her.

"Of course." She looked to Coach for a moment before her gaze settled on me.

"I'll think about it," I said, which caused her to exhale. Had she seriously held her breath? "I'll come back before I leave today."

"Thank you. I'll share more details then."

She seemed relieved. I had no idea she had such a competitive streak. I'd never been asked to consult for the team before.

Coach gestured for me to follow. The hall didn't have much traffic since nearly everyone was at lunch.

"We're headed to my office," he murmured. "You haven't responded to some urgent texts."

"I turn my phone on when I get to the cafeteria. Mr. Moore is crazy about phones in class, and I don't take chances with detention."

"Maybe you can find a solution so you can be notified and still be stealth?"

Being out of touch for an hour for class or a couple hours for a game had never been an issue, though Tactical Operational Support could need me at some pretty odd hours. Something must've gone wrong.

While we walked, I fired up my phone since Coach couldn't give me details.

"You have your computer with you?"

"Of course."

"Good."

"Details?"

"It's above my clearance. If they've asked me to find you during the school day, it's got to be major."

We moved fast. It wasn't a run, but anyone watching might think we'd taken up power walking. I scrolled through texts from Lorenzo, but none of those offered details. I messaged him back: *Stand by. Getting secured.*

Once we got to Coach's office, I got to work. I pulled out my laptop and booted it up. I grabbed earbuds from my pack, jammed them into my ears and called Lorenzo Davenport, my main contact in TOS IT. I logged in to the TOS network as fast as I could.

"I'll leave you to this." Coach opened one of his desk drawers and pulled out a protein bar that he dropped on the desk. "In case you miss lunch completely."

"Thanks." I pointed at my ears to indicate my call connected. Coach nodded and left the office. "Doctor Possible, Winger here." I used the mandatory TOS greeting. Even after all these years, it never got old using my codename.

"Winger, glad D-Man found you. We've got a critical situation."

"Tell me."

"The mission Keys went on has gone very wrong," Lorenzo said, stress evident in his voice. That rarely happened. "We believe she's dead. That leaves Cocoon as the sole person on a keyboard, and she doesn't have the needed skills. We've got to plug you in and hope you can finish the decryption so she can complete the mission."

This was catastrophic. Claire, or Keys, was TOS's chief cryptologist and security expert. She didn't go into the field often. But, just as I had gone out to stop the hack on TOS's tracker chips, she would've been the best choice to masquerade as part of a hacking duo—especially if the agent had no skills. Knowing she might be gone saddened me. She was a friend and mentor.

"Where do I need to log in?" My voice quivered. I knew no one would judge the emotions, especially Lorenzo.

"Cocoon is on a laptop with the new undetectable network connection. I've already patched you in."

The undetectable network was one of the coolest things we'd deployed recently. It worked over wired and wireless connections in 94.3 percent of the test cases we'd run. It meant we could be on agents' computers almost anywhere without being detected by the host network, even if the computer itself was in use by someone else.

"Cocoon, Doctor Possible here," Lorenzo said. "I've got Winger connected to your laptop and comm channel."

"Don't be foolish like your partner. Finish the job." The male voice was distant but harsh, and I couldn't quite place his accent.

A new window opened on my screen, pushed to me by Lorenzo. I saw the strings of encryption from Cocoon's computer. This was hard-core security, on the level that protected the TOS network and other highly sensitive networks, like the defense department.

"This is complex work, and if I do the wrong thing, they're going to know I'm in here." Cocoon sounded frayed but not out of control. It could be an act for the people in the room with her. I'd never worked with Cocoon before, but other agents often played the part of being distressed to buy time.

"Cocoon, Winger here. I've got control over your computer. In case they're watching, keep typing because my keystrokes will display on your screen."

"Winger, Keys has done a lot of the work." Lorenzo quickly told me what Keys had done. This system was indeed complex if she'd already been working for a couple hours and wasn't in yet. Keys and I challenged each other often, so I knew firsthand the difficulty in designing something she couldn't break.

"Got it. Thanks, Doc."

I scanned the code and deployed some of the programs I'd designed to help me crack systems. I had ideas, based on what Keys had done, but I wasn't sure if I could get through the security if she couldn't.

I focused, worked through what I had in front of me, and used the information my programs provided.

Time seemed to speed by. I stole a look at the clock in the corner of my screen, and I'd already been at this for nearly forty-five minutes. How long would the people with Cocoon wait for this hack?

One of my programs popped up a notification that it found a potential exploit. I strengthened my programs based on things I learned, and it was exciting anytime they discovered a weakness.

"I think I've found something. Cocoon stop typing and just read the screen. I'll let you know when to start again." I worked quickly to read through the code the program had found.

Keys and I played this game often—see who could crack a code puzzle the fastest without running into traps and, possibly, destroying the encrypted information.

"Doc, what are we breaking into here?"

"It's need-to-know. For what it's worth, Keys and I don't know either. Cocoon will confirm when it's open, and I'll deploy malicious code to destroy it once she's clear."

"Understood."

Okay, blindly forward. Not the best way to work, but sometimes necessary.

There were a couple of possible exploits and I went to work on those. I let Cocoon know she should appear to be in deep thought and to resume typing.

I found a continuously changing password. It reset every twenty seconds.

And that was the key. I needed to force it to always use the same password so Cocoon could authenticate and unlock the system.

I looked around the host server to see what routines were actively processing—only 336. I created a quick script to show me what had a processing pattern.

It took less than a minute to find it—a table accessed at twenty-second intervals. The password had to come from there. The table, of course, had its own encryption. The routine that fetched the new password, however, had what I needed. The decryption code was there.

"Think I've got it," I said. "Stand by."

It only took another five minutes and I pulled out an upcoming password and rewrote the system to only use the one I'd picked.

"Okay. I've got the password." I read it out to Cocoon and told her I'd locked the system so she wouldn't have to worry about access.

"Well done, Winger," Lorenzo said.

"Gentlemen, it's done." She sounded confident with the

job complete. Hopefully the people she was with would approve.

"Let me see," said a man's faint voice. "Looks good," the same voice said after a few minutes.

I couldn't see the output. They must be logged in on a different machine.

"I'm downloading a copy for our analysis," Lorenzo quietly said. "Also adding our virus so the information is destroyed on your mark, Cocoon. Winger, you can sign off. Please contact me for a debrief this evening."

Lorenzo was my boss, so I wasn't going to ask further questions. "Understood. Let me know if you need anything else. Winger out."

I hung up, grabbed the protein bar from the desk, unwrapped it, and took a bite before I closed the laptop. I couldn't believe Keys might be dead. I leaned back in Coach's chair and closed my eyes while I chewed on the bar and tried to let the adrenaline drain away. I'd have to come up with a cover for why I didn't meet Eddie for lunch.

Suddenly the office door burst open and slammed shut. Startled, I fumbled getting to my feet.

Shit. A dude all in black, including a ski mask. What the hell? Talk about vintage bad guy. How'd he get in here? This school is secure as a fortress.

"Finally, Winger. We've wanted you for a long time now." The voice was low and menacing.

He rushed me before I could process that he'd used my codename. I assessed my options, and I didn't have many with the desk in front of me and the wall behind. My adrenaline surged. I wasn't going down without a fight.

I jumped up on the desk, sending papers flying to the floor. The guy grabbed at my legs and I kicked him square in the chest, which slammed him into the wall. A couple of framed pictures fell, shattering glass.

I used that moment to jump down and throw a right hook. He blocked the right, but I nailed him in the ribs with my left. His "oof" let me know I'd connected pretty well.

He shoved me back against the desk and I stumbled. His one-two punch struck me below the ribs and under my chin.

Out of nowhere he produced a knife and pinned me against the desk. The dude's eyes through the mask were crazed. I reached behind, grabbed the edge of the laptop, and swung the computer to knock the knife out of the attacker's hand. After getting both hands on the computer, I swung back as he grabbed his injured hand.

"Winger! Pepperoni!" I froze, laptop midair ready to come down. He'd used the secret word. "It's D-Man."

"What the hell, Coach?" I lowered the laptop slowly while he stripped off the mask.

"Remember I told you that you could be tested at any time." He grinned like he'd won a prize.

"You're sending me out of here with a bruised chin." I rubbed where his fist had impacted in an effort to dull the pain. "What'll people think?"

"Maybe you took a puck to the face this morning and the impact left a bruise despite your helmet. You're a hockey player, no one will give it a second thought." He pulled the sweatshirt over his head, revealing the long-sleeve henley he'd been in before. "You did good. Up on the desk to give yourself options was a great choice. Those box jumps you're doing for stamina came in handy. And you want to talk bruises? I'll feel that kick in the chest for days."

Over the holidays Coach Daly and John, who worked with my parents and me on TOS assignments, had taught me some self-defense moves. After what I went through last fall during the tracker system hack, I wanted to know how to take care of myself better in case I ever needed to again.

I leaned against the desk and clutched the laptop while I calmed down. I laughed. It burst out of nowhere and it wouldn't stop.

"Theo?" Coach sounded like he wasn't quite sure what to do with my outburst.

"Come on, it's funny." I gasped for air. "I kicked you into a wall and it was okay. How many students get to do that to a teacher?"

TWO

"You're the best boyfriend," I said to Eddie as he hugged me from behind. We were done with classes for the day and at my locker. We had a little time before I had to go to MIT and Eddie had practice.

"Why do you say that?" He leaned on my open locker door while I sorted out what I needed to take for tonight's homework.

"Let's see. On the top of today's list would be the sandwich you left in my locker. Talk about a lifesaver. Without it, I might've eaten a book during history class."

"Can't have that. I'm pretty sure that's not on a hockey player's approved diet." He tried to not laugh, but he couldn't suppress a grin, and some giggles spilled out. "What happened to you anyway?"

I wanted to tell him that I'd lost a friend. Lorenzo had sent me an email earlier confirming Keys hadn't survived the mission. There were protocols to be followed before I could mention Keys's death to anyone who hadn't been involved—and then it'd be only with the proper clearances.

For now I had to bury it because this wasn't the time or place to work through any of that.

"Mrs. H happened." I dropped a couple textbooks into my backpack, along with two library books I'd grabbed during study hall because I had a paper to write. "She talked my ear off. She kept going on about how I needed to help the team with the competition they've entered."

"For an hour? She must've laid it on thick."

"It's worth some significant cash. Thing is, I don't know how to teach what I know. I just know it. And the stuff they'll build, and what they have to crack, will be way too easy for me. It'll be like it's not encrypted at all."

"Condescending much?" Eddie's expression clouded over.

"What? You know what I do. I work on systems way beyond what any of them would've seen in class." Truth was that what I worked on was further than anything they could've possibly seen, anywhere. My cover story was that I had my own consulting firm and when anyone asked specifics I simply said, "It's confidential because of nondis-closure agreements." It worked well as a lie rooted in some sort of truth.

"You can't be the only you out there," he said, tone softening.

I grabbed the locker door and Eddie moved so I could close it.

"You're right," I relented. There were certainly other teenagers with similar skills. "But, if there was someone like me here, don't you think Mrs. H would know it, especially if they were on her team?"

"Maybe. But, you don't have to be a dick about it." Leave it to Eddie to knock me down a peg or two. "Are you going to help?"

That was the question of the afternoon. We headed to the parking lot since Eddie needed to get to the pool for practice. There weren't many people around. Most students tore out of school after the last bell. We had a little time, so we didn't rush.

"I'm already uncomfortable with the teaching aspect. And this is just short of being a ringer. It seems like a fine line between coaching and telling them how to just do the work. It's not good sportsmanship. It'd be just as wrong as if she were in the room during the competition guiding them. It'd be like putting Crosby on our hockey team or Phelps on the swim team."

"Yes and no."

"What?" I said it louder than I meant to. "How can you say that? Would you want to compete against Phelps?"

"No. Not exactly. What if a student here had the same skills you've got? Could they not be on the team and compete? If we had a swimmer better than the entire team, but was eligible to compete, should he be turned away? Same thing if an opponent's team had an amazing winger. Your D, center, and goalie would have to compensate for that."

"But—"

"You're a student at this school." Eddie was on a roll. "You're good with a computer, probably better than anyone else. Maybe there's someone like you at a competing school, and by being part of our team, you'll balance things out."

I stopped suddenly, which forced Eddie to do the same. "You're kinda brilliant, you know?"

His huge smile and raised eyebrow made my heart flutter.

"Sometimes, yeah." He craned his head down to plant a kiss on my lips.

A huge crash made us both jump. We looked around and saw nothing. It had to have come from the adjacent hallway. We traded concerned glances and jogged to the intersection to see what'd happened. Another smaller crash sounded when we rounded the corner.

At the far end of the hall, someone was shoved into a classroom, and another student closed the door behind them. A backpack, computer, and books were scattered across the floor.

"Come on." I grabbed Eddie's hand to pull him along as I headed toward the problem.

"Hang on." He resisted my efforts to move. "We should just get someone."

"We don't know what'll happen if we have to wait. You heard that racket."

He relented and we moved quickly down the hallway. The shouts got louder. This hall was deserted, so no one would hear the commotion except us. We stopped at the door. Through the small square window, I saw Wes Lockly, the school bully, holding some other guy by his jacket. I didn't know his name, but he was a senior like Wes.

I pulled open the door. "What the hell are you doing, Wes?"

If Eddie had issues with my action, he didn't show it. Wes and I had gotten into it once when I was a freshman, but I came out on top. I suspected with my new defensive skills, it'd be even easier if it came to that. Wes, though, tended to steer clear of jocks or anyone else who could take him.

Wes shoved the other guy into the first row of desks. One flipped over as the guy struggled to keep his balance.

"What's it to you, Reese?" he asked, looking over his

shoulder at us. "Why don't you and your boy just mind your business?"

"Your boy?" Eddie gave me an incredulous look.

Eddie and I stepped fully into the room but left the door open. Wes didn't show any signs of backing down, even though the odds were against him. Although it wasn't clear if Wes's target would be any good in a fight.

"Let him go." I didn't want to drag this out for too long.

"He owes me homework. If I don't get it in, Carlyle's gonna call my dad."

"And I told you, I was done at the end of last semester." The other guy spoke with a surprising amount of determination in his voice.

Wes made a fist and reared back but couldn't connect the punch before I stepped in and yanked his arm behind his back. He grunted in pain as he squirmed to get loose, which made me only hold him tighter. Once again, what I'd learned this summer came in handy.

"You wanna die, Reese? Let me go and I'll forget this."

"How 'bout you shut up?" Eddie stepped between Wes and the other student, who used the distraction to make a hasty retreat from the room without another word. While Eddie had nearly a half foot on me, he towered even more over Wes. "You're going to leave that guy alone. I'd suggest spending your free time with your homework."

"I'm gonna get you both." Wes didn't have much bravado left even though he threatened us.

I pulled back on his arm more and made him wince. "I could break this in two places right now if I wanted to. Just keep talking."

I looked to Eddie, who stared at Wes in a standoff that lasted longer than I expected it to since Wes had no help.

"Fine," Wes finally resigned.

I spun him around and pushed him toward the door. He stumbled a bit before he found the traction to stay upright.

"You two can't always be together. Watch your backs." He took off. His empty threats hung in the air.

"You're sexy in a standoff," I said, looking over at Eddie.

"And you're pretty badass." He stole a look at his watch. "Seriously? Breaking his arm?"

"I've got skills you've never seen." I winked at him, and he shook his head in disbelief, which was exactly what I wanted.

"I gotta go." He broke into a run to get out to his Jeep. "See you tonight," he called over his shoulder.

At my bike, which was the sole bike locked up on the rack because it'd gotten too cold for most people to ride, I noticed Wes. He stood by his car and stared at his phone. He alternated between poking the screen and shaking the device. He looked like he might throw it across the parking lot. Between technology issues and homework, it appeared he was having a bad day. For someone else I'd go offer tech support, but I let karma have its way with him.

THREE

IT TOOK thirty to forty minutes to cover the six miles to MIT. I loved the ride, which cut through a few different areas of the city—some residential, some industrial—and I got to go over two rivers. It relaxed me, especially on sunny, clear days like this, even though sunset had started already.

So far it'd been a fairly mild winter with temperatures that didn't get too cold, and there'd been very little snow. I never cycled with snow or ice on the ground or if the temperature went below twenty-five. While I liked to ride, there were times it wasn't worth it. This afternoon's midthirties, though, felt good.

Besides the rivers, one of my favorite spots along my route was the windmill on Alford Street. It sat on some nicely landscaped property that happened to belong to the Boston Water and Sewer Commission. The first time I'd come upon it, I thought it must be inside a park because the area seemed too nice to belong to a city utility. Days like today, the sun glinted off the blades, giving it a bit of a glow. If you looked just right beyond it, you could see a bit of the Mystic River.

As I approached, everything aligned to make the windmill strikingly beautiful. I stopped and looked up to watch the three blades turn. I pulled my phone from my pocket and snapped off a few pictures, which caught the blades at various angles. I wished I were a better photographer because there were probably cool shots here that I couldn't conceive.

A wave of tremendous sadness came out of nowhere and crashed down on me. Even bundled in a couple of layers to protect me against the chill, I felt goose bumps rise on my arms.

Keys had been a musician in her spare time, which is where she'd originally got the nickname that became her codename. When we first got to know each other last summer while I interned at TOS HQ, she told me she'd gotten into computers because of music.

She'd caught my confused look. I couldn't put computers and music together. I knew computers could be used to make music, of course. I couldn't make the leap to her current job, though.

I learned the connections between mathematics and sound in geometry class. The teacher spent some time on Pythagoras's work where he derived musical tones from geometrical patterns. And, of course, math had a significant role in cyber security and computers because of the logic and algorithms involved.

Keys taught me about connections between music and math that I'd never thought about. One of the best puzzles she ever gave me had an encryption algorithm based on the percussion in a Rush song, something called "La Villa Strangiato."

I'd never heard of the band or the song, but I loved

visiting her office because she played great music. Before she'd given me the puzzle, she played the song in the background a few times while I visited in her office. I hadn't picked up on the connection. While I did crack the puzzle, it'd have gone much faster had I caught on to the patterns from that song. I was embarrassed I'd missed it, but fascinated at how she'd used the music to build the security. After that, I started using music sometimes too.

I once based some cryptography off the piano from a Sara Bareilles song, guitar from Prince, and cello off a tune from the musical *Spring Awakening*. The odds of anyone layering those specific elements together as a potential way to break security were low. After stumping her for a few days with that, I usually based a part of any encryption I sent to her on some eclectic combination of song parts. I ensured that I didn't get into any coding patterns that would be noticeable because she would've been quick to exploit them.

I should use music more often to honor Keys.

Before I pocketed my phone, I saw the time and realized I needed to hustle. I'd spent too much time and ran the risk of being late. It wasn't long before I pedaled over the Mystic.

Barely halfway across, sobs suddenly heaved through me. Tears flowed and I struggled for breath as rough sounds escaped my mouth. The cold air mixed with the tears and made it hard to see, so I pulled over. I quaked as the emotional tidal wave continued. The goose bumps at the windmill hadn't prepared me for this.

I got off the bike and pulled it out of the bike lane and onto the pedestrian area. Slowly, I went to the bridge railing so I could lean the bike against it. I looked out over the water and wondered if I'd broken something, because the tears wouldn't stop. The intensity rocked me unlike anything I remembered feeling, even in the aftermath of the tracker case.

I dropped my helmet next to the bike. With no tissues or even loose clothing to wipe my eyes with, I took off the beanie I wore under the helmet. I couldn't stop any of it— the tears, the sniffles, the occasional anguished sound. Looking at the river only seemed to make it worse. The calm, serene beauty in the late afternoon light directly opposed the way I felt.

"Are you okay?"

The question startled me and I turned around fast. Two women on bikes looked at me. What would they think of me?

I nodded and tried to pull myself together. "Yeah." My voice cracked twice on the small word.

The women, who looked vaguely college age, looked at each other and then back to me. The one who'd asked the question spoke again. "You're not going to hurt yourself, are you?"

That surprised me, but then it made total sense. Crying teenager on a bridge, of course they'd ask that.

"No. No way." Even I didn't believe that, because I sounded so bad. I looked to the sky and tried to center myself. "I lost a friend today and... it kind of all hit me right here."

They got off their bikes and came closer.

"Do you need to call someone to come get you?"

Somehow a bit of a chuckle broke through the tears. "I actually need to get going. I've got class." She looked confused. "I take computer-science courses at MIT."

"Oh." And now she sounded surprised. "You don't...." She trailed off.

This actually improved my mood a lot. "It's okay. I'm sixteen. I think you were going to say I don't look like a college student."

"You're right." She smiled. "Do you want to ride with us? We're headed to campus too."

I wiped my eyes again since the waterworks tapered off. "No, thanks. I need to make sure I'm done. Cold air and wet eyes don't mix."

"Yeah." They gave knowing nods. "Sorry about your friend."

"Thanks," I managed to say.

"We'll get going," the woman holding the bikes said. "We wanted to make sure nothing was going to happen to you."

I swallowed, determined to speak. "Thanks. I appreciate you stopped, you know, just in case."

We all smiled and they rode away. I pulled out my phone. I had to talk to my counselor tonight. I couldn't have outbursts like that.

"Shields. Winger here."

"Winger. Everything okay? We don't have an appointment today." Her calm voice, perfect for the kind of work she did, helped pull me back together. I couldn't imagine her ever angry or even stressed.

I explained about the mission and my breakdown on the bridge. I'd go into specifics later, but I'd said enough. With all the talk, I felt better.

"I'm free all evening. Let's talk after you debrief with Doctor Possible. Call me when you're ready."

"Thanks, Shields. I'll talk to you later."

I looked over the river and put the phone away. A couple of deep breaths and some water from my bottle and I could go again. If I hustled, I'd make it in time, and I suspected the extra physical effort would clear my head even more.

FOUR

I GOT HOME near six and found Dad in the kitchen, cooking at the stove. It wasn't a total surprise, we all cooked from time to time, but somehow it wasn't the scene I expected to come home to, especially since I thought he'd be on assignment for a couple more days.

"Hey!" I dropped my backpack next to the island and shared a quick fist bump with Dad. I took my usual hangout place in the kitchen, sitting on the counter.

"Hey. How's it going?"

"Bad day. Weird stuff."

"Weird? How so?" He drained some spaghetti into a colander in the sink.

"Missed lunch because Doc—" I stopped short since I didn't know Dad's clearance on the mission. "And, um, broke up a fight. Got asked to help the computer-science club at a competition in a couple weeks."

He stood at the sink with his back to me and shook the pasta. "I don't know where to start with that." He looked over at me as if trying to gauge how I actually felt. "I guess

I'll start with the easy one. I'm glad you stopped a fight. Everything okay with that?"

"Yeah. Wes is a jerk. Caught him while he picked on some guy about homework. Eddie and I happened on it. The training that Coach and John gave me helped put a quick end to it."

Dad turned from the sink with a smile. "You didn't hurt him, I hope."

"He might take some aspirin tonight, but no permanent damage."

He nodded and had a proud *that's my boy* sort of look that he got when I made choices he liked. "And what's this with the competition?"

I gave him the rundown, along with what Eddie and I talked about. He listened and stirred the noodles into the sauce.

"Are you going to do it?"

"I talked with my prof after class to make sure he approved the time away and to see what he thought. He said it seemed like a great opportunity to apply my knowledge in a different way. I get Eddie's point too—that I'm eligible to be there. I feel weird helping like that since I can likely code circles around all of them."

"Can I give you some advice?"

"Sure."

"I think it's a great idea that you can share what you know. Don't do the work, but help the team see how to do it themselves. Remember how much you enjoyed the time you spent with Lorenzo and the IT team during the summer? They taught you and you taught them. Passing on skills is a great thing to do. Maybe you build scenarios for them to hack as part of the lead-up to the competition and coach them on the processes to crack them."

Keys came to mind again. The puzzles we'd traded made me better. Anytime she'd take more than a day to crack something I'd sent her had thrilled me. The longer we'd worked together, the more I created encryption that slowed her down.

In terms of the competition, Mrs. H had said sort of the same thing as Dad. He put a really good spin on it by reminding me of the summer. If I taught right, by the time the competition arrived, I might not have to do anything on-site.

"You want some dinner? I made more than enough." Dad went to the cabinet to get plates.

"Sure." I hopped off the counter and went to the fridge to get a couple of sodas. "Where's Mom? And what's got you cooking?" I put the sodas on the counter and Dad served the pasta.

"I wasn't in the mood for takeout, so I cooked what we had on hand. Mom got called out earlier today. John told me when I got home. I missed her by less than an hour."

I grabbed forks before I moved the sodas to the table and joined Dad as he sat with the plates.

"Do you know how long you're here for?" I dug into the food and it tasted delicious.

"I don't have anything scheduled right now, so we'll see. I hope I'm here to see your game this weekend. It's been a few weeks since I've seen you on the ice."

"That'd be cool."

I liked it when Mom and Dad made it to games. It was awesome that as busy as they were that they *wanted* to be at the games and did it as often as they could. Our family had been what most people would call odd for just about as long as I could remember, but it was okay. I knew guys on the team whose parents never showed up.

My parents worked hard, and yet whenever we could, we did family stuff—whether it was them at my games, having dinner, or even a weekend camping trip sometimes. I had it good—different, but good—and I knew it.

"You mentioned something about Doc. Everything okay? They don't usually call you at school."

We held each other's gaze, and I worked to keep my emotions in check. I didn't want another outburst like I'd had on the bridge. Keys's death wasn't my fault, but it weighed on me.

"The mission completed, but—" What could I say that wouldn't violate security? "There were losses."

Dad put a hand on my shoulder. "I'm sorry. I can listen to whatever you can tell me. You should probably call—"

"Already done. We'll talk later tonight."

"Good." Dad squeezed before he went back to his food. He knew when to push me and when to let me manage on my own. Thankfully he knew not to push on this.

The tracker hacker case had taught me to not keep things bottled up. I talked to Mom and Dad more about TOS now—always mindful of clearances. I also had a great counselor with Shields. I only knew her by codename, and we never talked by video, only voice. I didn't have to edit for her because she had maximum clearance. It wasn't the usual doctor/patient privilege, though. If she had any concerns about my mental health, she could contact Lorenzo, since he's my boss, or, since I was a minor, my parents. She'd helped me a lot in the past few months to resolve what'd gone down in Denver, and with how to deal with keeping so many secrets from people like Eddie.

"What's happening for you tonight?"

"I've got a paper I need to start outlining. I've also got

calls with Lorenzo and Shields. I hadn't thought beyond that."

Dad raised an eyebrow. "Where are you with *Mr. Robot*?"

I thought for a moment. "Three episodes behind."

"We're even. Want to watch one or two? I've got nothing pressing."

I smiled. "Yeah! Maybe around nine?"

He nodded and we ate in silence for a bit—more like Dad ate and I scarfed, including a second helping.

We didn't watch much TV because all of us were busy with our own things, and frankly real life had enough drama. *Mr. Robot* had caught my attention because it was about a hacker, and I always liked to see how that played out on TV or the movies. I had quite a collection—from *Hackers*, *Sneakers*, and the original *TRON* to stuff like *The Net*, *Disclosure*, and *Johnny Mnemonic*. *Mr. Robot,* though, was the most realistic fiction I'd seen.

Dad got into it because he caught part of an episode I had on. We watched together when we could, or talked about it when we were both at the same episode. Clever didn't begin to describe the show, and its twists were pretty epic. We ended up with a running joke after each episode. Dad would always ask that I never become Elliot, and I'd assure him that if someone were going to take up residence in my head I'd give Henrik Zetterberg first dibs.

He stood and cleared the dishes while I finished my soda.

"I'll get the dishes." I went to the sink and nudged Dad out of the way. "You cooked after all. It was good too and exactly what I needed."

"It was nothing special, but thanks." He left, and I got

the water going to rinse things off before loading them into the dishwasher.

Once I had the dishes done, I took my pack and headed upstairs.

FIVE

After I logged in to TOS, I got a message from Lorenzo saying I could ring him when I was ready.

"Doctor Possible, Winger here," I said. His face filled the screen and he looked haggard, which was far from normal. Even if he worked long hours on a project or mission, his normal demeanor was upbeat. Keys's death no doubt weighed on him.

"Hey, Winger."

"You okay?"

"Been a long day." Lorenzo shrugged and rubbed his hand across his forehead and eyes.

"I'm sorry, man. I can't imagine—"

"It's been a long time since we lost someone from IT," he said. "We almost lost you in Denver and now Keys is gone. It's... hard."

"How can I help?" I wished I were in the same room with him, to offer a hug or something.

"That's part of what we'll talk about. Let's start with debriefing on what went down today."

We talked through the mission and what I'd done,

covering what worked well and what didn't. Lorenzo also told me that overall, we were successful and the malicious code he'd deployed had done its job. We finished that part of our discussion pretty quick.

"Before I tell you the new mission, I want to ask about having you take on more responsibility. I've already talked to Red Hat, and she agreed that you'd be ideal." Red Hat, a.k.a. Joanna, was Lorenzo's boss. "With Keys gone, you're our top encryption expert. No one else on the team has the knowledge needed to replace her leadership."

Whoa. What? Security and gadgets were my dual specialties, but to lead?

"Um... I...." Words escaped me. I hadn't seen this coming. I assumed Lorenzo would take over until they found someone to replace Keys.

"We don't want you to have to deal with mission assignments like she did. You'd oversee our encryption technology and research so you'd continue to push the security team to find new, better ways to do things."

"I don't know what to say."

"Think it over. Talk with Defender and Snowbird." Of course Dad and Mom would have to be involved. "They have to approve it too since it puts you in a different status. If necessary, it can be interim until we find someone with the right qualifications for the job."

"Will do." It was one thing to work as part of the team, but to lead? Did I know how to do that? "I can talk to Defender. Snowbird is deployed. Thanks for even asking. It means a lot that you think I could even begin to fill in for Keys."

"You've earned it for sure." Lorenzo gave me a sad smile, which made me want to say yes if only to help ease his mind. "I know we really shouldn't ask you. It's easy to forget you're a teenager because you're so good at what you do. We've got redundancies across the staff in many places in case anything happens. In this case—" His voice faltered and he cleared his throat. "You don't need to worry about that part. Let's talk new mission."

I nodded and he displayed a destroyed laptop on my screen.

"This laptop was in the possession of an executive with the North American Electric Reliability Corporation. It was taken while a team posing as police in Houston detained him. As you can see, the laptop's self-destruct initiated. However, analysis showed that data was copied in the seconds before the hard drive's destruction. They stole a multilayered encrypted key. If it's decrypted and used, it would allow the user unrestricted access to the North American electrical grid."

"Why would something like that be created? It sounds way too dangerous."

"It's one of many fail-safes." He reappeared on-screen. "There are only four keys. No one's supposed to know who has them, and they're distributed on a rotating basis. The theory is the key holders could manage the electrical system to stabilize the grid if something compromised or hindered personnel on a national or regional level. Investigations are underway on how the security breach occurred since this has worked for years."

"Are they taking steps to regenerate the keys to negate the one that was stolen?"

"I wish I could say yes." Lorenzo frowned, clearly not happy with the security lapse. "The keys are automatically regenerated and distributed every forty-five days. The system's designers never took into account that they might need to generate keys on the fly, or that someone could subvert their security and steal a key. Apparently a security protocol either failed or fell victim to a hack because it shouldn't have been possible to copy the key off the laptop."

"All right. So we need to redesign the system that creates the keys?"

"I wish." More of his frustration became apparent. "I'm told there's a qualified team at work on that. For now, we're one of the agencies tasked with recovering the key before it can be cracked."

"Have we put bots out looking for the file?" I leaned back in my chair and looked at the information Lorenzo shared across three of my screens.

"Here's everything that's been deployed over the past few hours."

"With the file in the hands of someone who managed to get it off the laptop, they're going to be smart enough to hide it well."

"Exactly."

"We need to design something that can sniff beyond firewalls, as well as into the deep and dark web," I continued. "Given the encryption schema, I wouldn't be surprised if they're going to have multiple groups trying to decrypt it. Let me see what kind of scripts I can create that are different from what's already gone out. One more thing, how is this key decrypted for use?"

"There's a decryption key that they didn't get. It self-destructed as it should have."

"At least something worked right." I rolled my eyes, and Lorenzo gave a partial smile. I'd hoped to coax a laugh out of him, but I didn't get it.

"I'll update you when I get more details. I'll drop all this into your working directory." Lorenzo sat quietly and looked into the camera for a moment before he continued.

"I'm trying to put something together for the people who worked with Keys. I'll let you know when and where. If nothing else, maybe you can virtually be there."

"I'd like that. And I'll talk to Defender so I can let you know about your offer."

"Thanks, Winger. Be careful, okay?"

"Will do." Lorenzo disconnected and left me sitting in silence.

I felt bad for him. His team had been through a lot in the past few months since the huge breach with the trackers.

I shuddered in my chair; emotions threatened again. Keys was laid-back, quick with a joke, but super serious about the work. I could get into a pretty intense zone when I worked, but nothing compared to watching Keys go methodically through a problem and start to build code around it.

I learned a lot from her. I'd asked her once why she chose TOS for a career when she could have been an amazing teacher or musician. "I teach people and help solve problems here," she'd said. I couldn't argue that point. I certainly got a lot from knowing her. Now TOS was asking me to carry on her work.

Did I know enough to do it?

I'd have to think on that. Later.

I had a lot to get through tonight. Sadly, *Mr. Robot* time with Dad would have to wait.

SIX

Two DAYS later I stood in Mrs. H's classroom to attend my first computer-science club meeting. To my surprise, the guy Eddie and I'd rescued from Wes was among the eight students present. Cullen Watson, a freshman I'd helped last fall, was also here.

When I'd accepted Mrs. H's offer yesterday, she told me the club had been prepping for the competition since October. She'd taught them various methods to encrypt and decrypt and how to test the entry they created.

As she introduced me, animosity filled the room. Given my low comfort level already, this didn't help my anxiety. It seemed Mrs. H didn't completely sell them on why she brought me in.

"Why do we need him?" one of the three girls asked. "Just because he goes to MIT doesn't mean he's better than us."

I held my tongue and let Mrs. H talk. I would've been happy to walk away from this so I could get back to my own projects.

"Actually, in terms of the goals of the competition,

Theo's better than all of us." Mrs. H leaned against the edge of her desk. "He's got practical, real-world experience. He'll make what we submit better, and he'll make you better at exploiting weaknesses."

"Let's see him crack what we've got, then."

"Good idea, Dean. Maybe it'll show you we can use his coaching. Theo, you game?"

The bullying victim had a name: Dean. If he recognized me from the other day, he gave no sign, but he seemed ready to test my skills.

"Sure. Let's do this." I sat down at one of the laptops in the classroom. It wouldn't be fair if I used some of the shortcut scripts I'd developed over the years. I'd show them exactly what I could do with no prep, much like they'd have to in competition.

"Let me update your school login so you can access our part of the network," she said.

"No need. I'm almost in." I looked up from the screen and we traded a smile.

In no time I accessed the network's admin. Some students gathered around to watch me work because I'd gotten into the network in less than a minute. Mrs. H typed on the computer at her desk and displayed my screen on the room's big monitor to allow everyone to easily see.

In another couple of minutes, I found what they'd built for the competition. The encryption job was decent, but I found a couple of exploitable flaws. Within fifteen minutes, I had the file of fake user data exposed on the screen.

"Really?" Dean asked, clearly frustrated. "We've worked weeks on that and you destroyed it like it was nothing."

I switched to a view of their code and walked up to the screen to point out how I got in. "This is how you get better.

Weaknesses are pointed out and you change your plan. What you've got is good. I assume it got to the point that not one of you could crack it on your own, because I see different coding styles in there, so you built on each other. But I've done this for years. I got my first job in cyber security when I was eleven."

That caused some chatter among the team.

"Why help us, then?" asked Jessie, a girl I had history class with.

"Mrs. H wants you guys to win. She thinks I can help."

"But what's the point if you're doing it for us?" Jessie crossed her arms across her chest and looked annoyed. "You could be a team of one."

Mrs. H had really not prepped them on anything. Maybe this was part of my team hazing. "I want to help you be better. Do you want to give it a go? Or should I walk away?"

Silence fell over the room. I don't think they expected to get a choice. Mrs. H didn't speak up, so she must've been okay with my tactics.

"Winning will look good on all of our college apps," Jessie said.

"And the money will help too, so we might as well," Dean said. His teammates nodded and murmured in agreement.

"Okay, then." I released a breath I hadn't realized I was holding. I'd won over some of them and hopefully I'd get the rest quickly. "I brought in some encryption puzzles that I designed. At the heart of each of these is a text file, so it's like what you've already built. I've got six, and they get progressively harder. Let's see what you can do with these."

I pulled my laptop out so I could drop what I'd created onto the network for the team to access. "I think you should work together like you would at the competition. And if you've got questions, I'll be here."

"We've got ninety minutes left," Mrs. H said from her desk, "so take seventy to work on these and we'll review with the rest of the time."

The team seemed to have a strategy in place already. Two of the guys and one of the girls were at keyboards while the other five were split up behind them. One wheeled a whiteboard over so they could write things out.

After fifteen minutes a horn sounded, which signaled that they'd cracked one. Some of them jumped, which forced me to suppress a laugh.

"Sorry. The sound of a goal score seemed appropriate."

That got grins from some of them before they went back to work. I was glad they'd gotten the first one so quickly. Mrs. H had been right about their skill level, and I pulled together my test modules based on that. The first one was slightly more difficult than what I'd cracked from them so there was hope. This teaching thing might be okay after all.

The team settled back into their work, and I made a secure connection so I could check in on some TOS stuff. I'd had some ideas for how to augment the bots I'd already deployed, and I wanted to get those out. The major objective for the bots involved evading security and tracking down the file. Whoever had the encrypted key wasn't likely to put it somewhere unprotected. We needed to not only look for signs of a transfer but to peek behind firewalls to see if we could find it.

That was tricky business. The bot had to be stealth and do its job. The ultimate problem Lorenzo and I talked this morning about was what could happen if copies were made. In theory, the file couldn't be copied without proper authorization. Since it'd already been removed from the laptop, it seemed a safe assumption that the thieves could've overridden other security features as well.

Another "goal" sounded and this time several of the students cheered.

"How'd you do that?" Jessie asked. "It changed while we worked. Like it knew it was under attack."

I closed the laptop and looked at them while Mrs. H got up and went behind them, looking at their screens. "Self-defense is a tool that's often used. Some of them are breakable, as you saw. Of course, the more you make the security react in unpredictable ways, the more difficult it is to break. It also means you can't leave too obvious of a backdoor like some coders want to do."

"But you left a backdoor in the first one," said one of the girls. It was a huge fail that I didn't get their names before I started. "It's how we got in."

"Exactly. It's not the smartest programming move, but it's always worth looking for." Time ticked down, but I wanted to push them forward.

"This is great," Mrs. H. said. "Try to get one more done before we break for questions and decide how we want to spend the next few days."

They got right back to work and I loved their eagerness. We'd moved past the initial awkwardness. Hopefully they saw I was really just a geek like they were.

They couldn't get the third puzzle done before the time expired. There were no signs of defeat among the team, though.

"Can we work on these for Friday?" asked the girl who'd called out the backdoor.

"It'd be cool to start the next meeting with all six unlocked. You can always ask me questions too. Catch me in the hall or email. Maybe think about what you see in these files that you can apply to what you're creating too."

"Could we win with what we built?" Jessie asked.

What was the right answer? "Maybe." I shrugged. "Mrs. H thought you had a solid entry. There are a lot of similarities between that first file I gave you and what you designed. You guys cracked that quick. We need to evolve what you'll submit so it's stronger, more like other samples I made you."

"We should totally do something that morphs," one of the guys who'd yet to speak said.

I grinned that I had them interested. Now I had to guide them on how to build something like it, or even better.

"We cracked his code," Cullen said. "We should dig into it to see how it works."

The team agreed with him. They were going down the right path without me saying anything. Maybe I was doing this right.

"So, um, listen," I said, bringing their attention back, "I messed up when we started. Can you please tell me your names? I know Cullen, Jessie, and Dean."

In short order I had the rest of the names. The other guys—Ryouta, Lars, and Nat—and the other girls—Alice and Li.

"Cool. Thanks. Good luck with getting the rest open by Friday."

None of them left the room. Instead they went back to their screens and worked. Impressive. I packed my stuff because I needed to get home to finish the bot upgrade and do my homework. I still needed to talk to Dad too.

I walked up to Cullen where he worked at a white-board. "Hey, man, got a sec?"

"Yeah, sure." He capped the marker and pointed at the door and I nodded. "Back in a minute, guys."

"How are you?" I asked once we were in the hall. "Things good?"

Cullen's dad had hired someone to change court records to make it appear he had custody of his son. Cullen had come to me to fix it, but I didn't want to add a second illegal hack. Ultimately Mom had TOS fix it. Since he was a freshman, we didn't cross paths often, so I wanted to catch up.

"Yeah, man. We've got a restraining order against Dad, and he goes to trial in March. He's got one of those ankle bracelets, so he can only go so many places right now."

"That's good. It's cool but unexpected to see you here."

"After all that went down, I wanted to learn more about computers, so I signed up for Mrs. H's beginners course. She moved me into the intermediate class after a few days and asked me to join the team. She says I see patterns in a way that makes this easier for me somehow. I don't totally get it, but some of it does seem easy." He chuckled. "But some of it seems really hard too. Jessie says I'm helping them, though, so that's cool."

I nodded and clapped him on the back. "A natural. Nice. That's how I started too. Some of it seemed so obvious, and then I enjoyed figuring out new stuff. I'll let you get back. I just wanted to say hi."

He nodded. "Later, man. See you Friday."

SEVEN

"So you're a teacher now?" Mitch asked as he, Eddie, and I wrapped up our work for the night on our history project. We'd practically become the three musketeers since we were together so much. Mitch was my best friend for years and my team captain. Luckily, when Eddie and I became a couple last year, he fit in perfectly with the friendship I'd already had. It probably helped that Mitch had a girlfriend, Iris, who hung out with us a lot too.

"I prefer to think of it like a coach. Mrs. H has taught them the basics over the past few months. I'm there to hone their skills. It's sorta like how we have specific coaches that work with the forwards, the defense, and the goalie."

Mitch nodded. "It's scary how much is in that brain of yours. When you're rich and running your own company, try not to forget about the rest of us."

"Maybe I'll just be a hockey player and keep the tech stuff for a hobby." I never liked talking about the future or my skills. It wasn't comfortable since my situation differed so much from my friends.

"Or you'll do both, and I'm gonna be right there. I won't

let you forget about me." Eddie leaned over from his perch on the bed to me in my desk chair and kissed me. It was hot how he had to stretch his already long body to reach me.

"Could you two adopt me, then?" Mitch asked, looking between us. That question would've been awkward from anyone but him.

"Why?" I asked. "If any of us are going to the big time, it's you."

College scouts had circled around Mitch all season in an effort to snag him. He gave an "aw shucks" look, which made me think he disliked talking about the future as much as I did.

Our phones all buzzed at the same time, which never happened. Before I could grab mine off the desk, they buzzed again, twice in rapid succession.

"What the hell is happening?" Mitch pulled his phone from his jeans. "Oh man," he said while he scrolled. "Did you guys get this stuff from Wes Lockly?"

Eddie looked stunned. "Did he blast the entire school?"

I said nothing as I read the email with the subject "I'm not a nice guy." There was no way Wes did this. Why would he incriminate himself with details of what he'd done to Dean and apparently other students over the past couple of months? I scanned the long and detailed message, which included the beating we'd saved Dean from the other day. Thankfully Eddie and I weren't mentioned.

"I knew he was a bully, but I had no idea he harassed so many people." Mitch looked up from the phone. "Didn't he try to beat you up freshman year when he found out you were gay?"

"Yeah," I said quietly while my brain worked to process all this. Not only was the email strange, but so were the extra vibrations our phones gave when it arrived. "Until he figured out I could defend myself."

"You should've seen him take Wes on the other day." Eddie animatedly moved his hands as if he were pulling someone's arm back. "He was badass."

"He's a hockey player, of course he's badass," Mitch said. "And how come I'm just hearing about this?"

"Because it was nothing. We heard a commotion and broke it up."

"Still, I like to know when my best friend is being a hero."

"Hardly heroic." I tossed my phone on the desk. "We were in the right place to stop Wes before he hurt that guy. Oh, and get this, that guy is on the comp-sci team."

"Did he thank you since he ran off while we held off Wes?" Eddie pocketed his phone. I was glad we moved on from the email.

"Nope. If Dean recognized me, he said nothing. In fact he's one of the guys not too happy I was there."

"All right, I gotta get going," Mitch said as he packed up. "We're gonna work on this more tomorrow?"

"Yeah," I said.

"Works for me," Eddie added.

Mitch wheeled his chair back to where it hung out in front of my desk, alongside two others.

"See you tomorrow." Mitch fist-bumped with Eddie. "Later, Mr. Badass." He fist-bumped me too.

"I'll walk down with you. I need to scavenge the kitchen. You want anything?" I looked to Eddie. "I'm thinking Nutter Butters."

"That works."

"Sure, pull out the food when I'm leaving." Mitch pretended to sulk.

"Come on, you goofball. You can have cookies for the road." We bounded down the stairs to the kitchen. It was quiet with the sliding doors to Mom and Dad's office closed. Dad must still be working, and John might still be in there too since it wasn't crazy late.

"You coulda kicked me out earlier, you know, so you and Eddie could do whatever." Mitch took a handful of cookies from the package I put on the counter. He immediately stuffed two in his mouth.

"No worries. We needed to do that work, plus he's gonna help me with some physics."

"Uh-huh." Mitch winked and I shook my head even though I hoped there would be less studying and more something else. "Physics. I'll catch you in the morning."

"Yup. Bright and early as usual." We fist-bumped again before he was gone out the front door.

Once he left, I went back through the kitchen, grabbed the cookies, and headed upstairs.

Before I got to my room, I heard the ping of my computer indicating access denied. I quickened my pace and found Eddie in my chair, at my keyboard.

"What're you doing?" I managed to ask calmly. I didn't like anyone at my computer unless I specifically put it in safe mode. He hadn't gotten in, but still. Why was he there?

"I wanted to print some stuff to go over." He pulled a thumb drive from the side of the monitor and showed it to me.

"We can plug your laptop into a monitor so we can just read a screen." I grabbed his laptop from the bed and pulled out a spare cord to make the connection.

"That works." He pocketed the thumb drive and pulled a chair around so we could see the screen. We spent the next hour going over the very boring topic of heat transfer.

I was lucky to have a boyfriend with science smarts. It doesn't click for my brain. He'd gotten me through chemistry and now he was doing the same in the Intro to Physics course.

Once we were done at the computer, we got situated, sprawled on my bed, with our books open. Instead of getting down to work and making me explain the recent lectures, he looked at me with concern. "You okay? Every now and then, you've been somewhere else tonight. I don't think it's work, though, because you don't have the 'I'm solving a problem' look."

Keys dominated my thoughts tonight, as she had been all week. I suppose I got too caught up in that and hadn't realized it. I decided to go for some partial truth. "One of my mentors from one of my clients died suddenly. We worked together often and she'd actually become more than a mentor. She was a friend—"

He put his arm across my back and pulled me to him. "I'm sorry. When did it happen?"

"I only found out today." Okay, I lied, but I wanted to include Eddie so he couldn't think I'd sat on this too long. "Sometimes I end up thinking about it and how quick it happened."

He held me tighter. I kept it together even though it'd be easy to cry in his arms. "We don't have to talk about it if you don't want to, but I'm glad you told me."

"Thanks." I kissed him and that comforted me. "Let's get to studying. That would make her happy."

"Okay, then." He smiled and made me start talking about what I'd learned.

After a couple hours, where we alternated between studying and making out, I finally had to kick Eddie out so I could do some other things. I needed to check on the bots

I'd deployed. I couldn't put off the talk with Dad any longer either.

"You wanna catch a movie Sunday afternoon?" Eddie asked while we stood by his Jeep in the driveway. John's car was still there, so he and Dad were at work on something.

I thought for a second. We had a game Friday night and Eddie was swimming Saturday afternoon, which I looked forward to. Sunday should be free unless something came up with TOS.

"If my clients stay quiet, then yes." My default answer. Eddie looked unsurprised. "Grab a bite after?"

The lights on either side of the garage sparkled in his eyes. "Maybe we won't actually go to the movie."

I craned my neck up so I could kiss his lips.

"See you tomorrow," he said as he got into his Jeep. He rolled his window down so I could stick my head inside and kiss him a few more times.

"Love you." I pulled out of the window and stepped back as he started the engine.

"Love you too."

I watched him drive off and waved once to him before he turned off the street.

That ended the normal part of the evening. Hopefully I'd get to sleep before midnight so I'd be fresh for practice. The good thing about the stamina drills was that it gave me more energy overall.

EIGHT

THE OFFICE WAS STILL CLOSED, so I rapped on the door. I had to get this talk done.

Dad opened the door but not wide enough for me to enter. "Hey. What's up?"

"Just need to talk before I go to bed."

"Can you give me ten minutes to wrap up a call?"

"Sure. It's confidential. You can come up if you want."

"Okay." Confusion clouded Dad's expression. It wasn't often that John didn't have clearance for the stuff I talked to Dad and Mom about. But in this case, the loss of Keys remained need-to-know until further notice, and I only had the okay to talk to them. "I'll be up in a bit."

He closed the door and I headed upstairs. I tidied up from the study session—chairs went back in their places and cookie crumbs got swept into the trash can.

I used my master power switch to turn on my other computers and monitors. My main terminal still displayed the security warning from Eddie plugging in the thumb drive. I had notifications in place to let me know anytime the system had something unauthorized connected to it, but the additional notice that the drive had a virus on it threw me.

Did Eddie know he had a virus? I pulled up the logs, which had a snapshot of the drive's contents. The report showed regular files I'd expect to see, but also a trojan designed to transmit the infected computer's data over the internet. But to where?

What was going on? Eddie had a virus. Weird email sent to my classmates.

I fired off a text to Eddie.

Bring that thumb drive to school tomorrow. My computer says it's seriously infected. I'll fix it for you.

While I waited for his reply, I brought up the email that was supposedly from Wes. From the headers it certainly looked like it came from his school account. There was some markup as well that triggered the additional phone notifications. With the lengthy cc list, it looked like all the students got it. The recipients didn't seem to include any teachers or administrators. Did they get a different version? Or was the intent to embarrass Wes to his classmates? A trace showed the school's server didn't send the emails, but the server listed as the originator didn't seem to exist now.

I knew how to do that. Did anyone else at school? Who else would want to trash Wes other than Dean and the other bullying victims? At least I'd find out what Dean's skills were over the next few days. Even if I discovered he could do this kind of prank, what should I do about it? In some ways it was really not my business, but it was also wrong.

My phone vibrated with a text from Eddie.

Great. Just what I need. Can you look at my laptop in the morning too and make sure it's okay?

Of course. Theo's tech support to the rescue!

Thanks. Love you!

Love back atcha.

A knock at the door and Dad's face popping up on one of my screens prompted me to close the email. I entered the combination on the keyboard to open the door.

"Upgrade?" Dad looked at the door as he came in. "How'd you know it was me?"

"Oh yeah, did it last week." I might have sounded too proud of the new tech. "Replaced one of the nails in the door frame with a tiny camera and added a controller in the doorknob so I can release it from here."

"Seems a bit lazy." Dad came in and took a seat across the desk, and we traded smirks.

"Not lazy, efficient." I gave it my best salesman voice before I revealed the truth. "I'm testing it out. It's part of updated security protocols for safe houses or agents' homes. I designed the software for the remote unlocking, which can be set up for any device on the internet and can be made to interact with the camera too."

"Well done. I think your room is better secured than most of the house."

I grinned. "I can fix that. I've got another one of these I can install." I opened the drawer and held up the nail camera. "Front door? Your office?"

"Promise you won't make it so we can't get in."

I made a dismissive sound. "Of course not. That'd be a bug. I don't do bugs."

He chuckled, which lightened my mood headed into what we had to talk about. "So what's up?"

I told Dad about Keys and Lorenzo's offer, and I even managed to do it with limited cracks in my voice.

"I'm sorry about Keys. She was pretty extraordinary. You doing okay? You don't sound good."

"It's hard... and weird." I took a breath. I've cried in

front of Dad many times, including because of TOS work. I still hated it because I thought I should have better control. "I mean she's a coworker, a mentor... a friend. And she's just gone. It's a little surreal because I didn't see her in person very much, but we worked together and taught each other a lot. I've already talked to Shields a couple of times now."

He was pleased. A slight smile appeared. "I'm glad you're talking to her. I know it's not easy keeping it inside when you're around your friends."

I didn't tell him that I'd sorta told Eddie. Dad's soothing voice pushed the right emotional buttons, though, and I couldn't stop myself from losing it. He got up, came over next to the chair, and wrapped me in an awkward sideways hug. The side of my head pushed into his stomach, and I wrapped one arm around him.

This was nowhere near as hard as I'd cried on the bridge the other day, but it was another release. I pushed myself out of the chair so I could get a better hug. I'd thought I'd cried all this out during my talks with Shields, but my heart had other ideas.

Dad held on until I let him go. I looked around and, once again, had nothing to wipe my eyes on, so I used the sleeve of my sweatshirt to dry my face.

"You know, it wouldn't hurt to keep tissues in here. They're always handy." I caught Dad's slight smile as I pulled myself back together.

"You're probably right."

"Better?"

"Yeah."

"This promotion." He ran his hand through his hair and across his forehead—a sure giveaway the idea troubled him. "I have no doubt you can do the job—but you know your mom and I think school, hockey, Eddie, and being a somewhat normal teenager's got to be in the mix too. Do you want the job?"

I spun around in my chair—my favorite thing to do when I didn't have an instant answer. I stopped after a couple twirls to face Dad. "I feel like I always learned more from Keys than she did from me. I don't know how I'm supposed to replace her."

"Lorenzo wouldn't have offered the job if he didn't think you could do it. But you should talk to him about your reservations, or simply decline if you don't think you're ready for it."

"You're going to let me take it?"

Silence said a lot, especially combined with that head rub before. "I'm conflicted like you are, but for different reasons. If you say you want to take it, I don't think I'd say no. You're more than capable of making your own decisions, and you know what our expectations are. I know you'll push yourself to do an excellent job with anything you decide to do." He sighed. "I worry you're not a kid enough. You need to do more stuff like you did tonight with Mitch and Eddie."

"That was homework, though."

"But your friends studied with you, so even though you worked, I'm sure you guys goofed off too. I don't want you to become the kid who stays holed up in his room all the time. That's not healthy. And I'm—" The abrupt stop wasn't like him, and neither was the sadness that fell over his face. "I've got to be honest, and I know your mom feels the same. We're scared of losing you. We're very aware that you were in a lot of danger on the tracker case. I still have nightmares about aiming my gun at you. Now you've been offered the chance to take over for someone who died in the line of duty. Nothing about this is an easy choice."

For a moment I thought it was my turn to hug Dad,

because he looked on the verge of crying. He kept it together, though.

"I don't want to tell you no, because you're responsible enough to make the decision. Make sure it's what you want right now and consider the time ramifications. I don't want you to get to my age and wonder what you did with your childhood." He paused again, but I could tell he hadn't finished. "You're so talented, Theo. You're going to be able to do whatever you want in life. There's no reason to do so much now if you don't want to."

We looked at each other and I finally nodded. "You know, I kinda hoped you'd give me the answer."

He looked like he was about to roll his eyes, which made us both laugh. "No you didn't."

I shrugged. He was right, of course. "I'll think about it some more, especially what you said. I'll talk to Lorenzo too."

He nodded and stood. "We can talk more if you want, anytime. It's a big step, and I'm proud that you do the kind of work that gets you that offer." I nodded as he spoke. I didn't know how else to take the high praise. "You headed to sleep soon?"

"Yeah. Just a couple things to check on first." I turned to the keyboard to get started.

"All right. Good night."

"Night. Thanks, Dad."

He smiled before he walked out and closed the door.

NINE

WES SKIPPED SCHOOL ON FRIDAY. The email was the topic of the day in the hallways, and several people asked me if I could send emails like that and if I had any idea who did. No one believed Wes had done it.

The only time it didn't come up was the computer-science team meeting. When I arrived, I found the team working and I asked about their progress. They'd been busy and had cracked the third puzzle. They were eager to talk about the fourth one because it repeatedly blew up on them.

"We weren't expecting that," Jessie said. "And it keeps happening. We couldn't do anything to avoid it. I think we tried five or six different scenarios."

"It was five." Alice held up her tablet filled with notes. "I made notes so we wouldn't repeat our mistakes."

"Want to show me what you're doing?"

"It's sneaky, though, because the trigger isn't just in one place." Alice came forward with her tablet. "We'd repeat things that worked, but then get shut down at a different point."

"Exactly." I raised my eyebrows at them. "Now how do you get by it?"

The team broke up, but in different groupings than the other day. I liked that there were more people on terminals. For the tournament, everyone could be at a computer, or they could put themselves in groups. Mrs. H and I went among different groups and talked with them to find out what their strategies were. I offered guidance where I thought appropriate. Each of them had a good grasp of the theories involved. It only took about half an hour before they cracked number four, which they did by working simultaneously from three terminals.

"Great teamwork. Sometimes that's what it takes to get the job done effectively. I'm not sure if we'll run into anything like that at the competition, but it's good to be prepared."

"All right." Mrs. H got our attention. "Instead of cracking another of Theo's modules, I want us to take a look at the file you're creating for the other teams to hack." She brought up the code on the big screen. "Theo, do you want to discuss your suggestions?"

I brought up the code and the students settled into their seats. I focused on where I thought they had weaknesses and the principles that made those areas exploitable. Preparing to talk to the team had been a great way to decompress last night after some work on the TOS bots to make them more robust.

I asked them to tell me about the vulnerabilities they discovered in the puzzles I'd designed and how they found them. I underestimated what the team knew, and especially Dean. The more he talked, the more I thought maybe he did send out all that stuff about Wes.

"Okay." I focused on Dean. "Given your analysis of

problem four, how would you suggest rebuilding the team's security protocols so I can't crack them?"

"Uhm. Well, we could create something like you did, but I'd want to make it even stronger." The distressed look on Dean's face made me feel bad that I'd singled him out. "I've been looking at problem five and had some ideas based on it."

Dean walked up to the board, and I moved the big monitor out of the way. He looked like he wanted to keep himself from taking up too much space. Once he started writing, though, his speech became stronger, like he'd found his groove. His ideas were good, and if they decided to build what he outlined, they'd be in much better shape.

They all studied the board while Dean returned to his seat. No one looked confused.

"A couple of questions," I finally said when no one else spoke up. "Given you were able to show us this, why haven't you cracked number five yet?"

"I just haven't," he said abruptly. I hadn't expected the defensiveness, and his body language told me he probably lied about that.

"Okay. Not a problem. Consider this, though...." I went over and grabbed a marker to annotate what he'd written. "This subroutine could become a problem and so could this one."

As I wrote, my watch pulsed and the screen flashed the word *icing*. My phone's low-level defenses were pinged. It could be nothing since I monitored incoming traffic more than necessary. I'd check the logs later to see if I needed to modify anything.

"How would you secure those?"

Three people initially talked over each other. Each of

them, and eventually Dean, offered up a slightly different solution on the problem.

"Great." I put the marker down. "Good work, Dean and all of you." He shrugged and slumped down in his chair. "How about spending the rest of today working together to create this type of security for your file? If you can, spend time this weekend on it too since we've only got a week to go before the competition. It'd be awesome to see something Monday afternoon."

"Can we ask you questions over the weekend?" Jessie asked.

"Of course."

The team circled around and talked while I grabbed my laptop and went to my usual desk. I pulled up my phone's logs, which I stored on my secure server at home. It was a valid warning. Someone tried to access my phone, like they were testing the security—similar to how someone might jiggle a doorknob to see if it's locked. My phone used the school Wi-Fi, along with the hundreds of other student and staff phones.

My phone wasn't named anything obvious, though—

01001101010111001001000000010010000

01101000011011110110110011001100101

—and *if* anyone read binary, it would simply translate to *My Phone.*

It could be nothing more than someone seeing if they could get data off a stranger's phone. The school used secure Wi-Fi—far more secure than most homes. Two years ago I'd recommended an upgrade to the principal under the guise of making sure people who used it wouldn't be susceptible to identify theft. And that wasn't a lie; it had been a wide-open Wi-Fi connection before my changes. Of course, I had ulterior motives too. I needed the security so I could do TOS work if necessary. Everyone else simply benefited from it.

In this case, someone inside this network had pinged my phone. That didn't make sense, not unless the network had been compromised.

My watch pulsed stronger this time. *Penalty* displayed on the face.

"Aw, fu—" Dean slammed his fist on the desk but kept the rest of the word in his mouth as he sent a guilty look toward Mrs. H's desk. "Sorry." The outburst was a surprise. I didn't know he had that in him.

"What happened?" I went to his desk and Mrs. H also came over. My phone could wait. The "penalty" message meant someone had triggered security countermeasures. If something more serious happened, I'd get a "misconduct" message.

"Nothing." He jabbed at the corner of the keyboard. "Just need to reboot."

Once I got behind him, I saw the familiar angry emojis across his screen.

How was that possible? Dean had triggered my phone's defense protocol. He'd shown solid skills a few minutes ago, but I hadn't expected this level from anyone in here.

"Jeez, Dean, what'd you do?" Alice peered over to see his screen.

Dean looked at me, and I raised my eyebrow at him.

"I don't know. Must've tripped something in problem six." His look shifted between defiant and scared.

"You're supposed to be on the file encryption," Jessie chastised him.

"You should switch machines. This one will need to be recovered." I closed the lid on it and we stared at each other for a moment. "I'm afraid that was left over from a school project," I said to Mrs. H, who stood next to me. "I'll make sure the machine is fixed."

"That must've been a hard-core trigger," Jessie said. "I'd love to learn how to do that."

"We can look at that if there's still time once your encryption for the competition is complete." I circled back to the front of the class. This wasn't the time to deal with Dean. "We wouldn't want to use that sort of defense in competition because you wouldn't want to take out a competitor's computer."

"But that would be spectacular." Jessie's enthusiasm and her competitive streak were cool.

"Spectacular, yes, but against the rules." I turned as Mrs. H spoke while walking back to her desk. "The encryption designed cannot disable a computer. However—" She paused until she got to her desk and brought up something on her screen. "—it can, and I quote, *sound an alarm, and display a message indicating the computer is disabled. However, the message must be able to be cleared with a simple reboot of the computer.*"

"So we could do it?" Jessie held on to the idea, and Alice looked between me and her.

"I can show you the principles." I walked back to the whiteboard. "It's on you to figure out how to write it."

"And you'll have to show me that it can be cleared per the rules," Mrs. H said. "We don't want to get disqualified."

"Show us, please. It might be the edge we need," Alice pleaded like this mattered more than anything else.

I could throw a lot of information at them related to this. I suspected Dean could write it for them given that he tripped my protections. For the rest it might be over their skill level. I spent the next twenty minutes going over the basics, taking questions.

My watch lit up with a notification from Lorenzo, and it said he needed to talk as soon as I finished. That, unfortunately, meant I had to let Dean go without talking to him. It turned out he had no desire to talk to me either because he bolted from the classroom when Mrs. H dismissed the team.

TEN

I LOVED Saturday afternoons in the dead of winter because I got to hang out at the aquatic center a couple of times a month for swim meets. Eddie's swim season ran from mid-December into mid-February, and he attended my Friday games and I went to his Saturday meets.

Mitch and his girlfriend Iris were with me, as usual. This became our thing at the start of this swim season. It's not a well-attended sport at our school. When I told Mitch that sometimes I was the only student in the stands who didn't seem forced to be there by their parents, they decided to support Eddie too. It was cool of them to do that. Eddie's parents were usually here too, but they were missing this one.

"Look at him." Iris poked me in the ribs and subtly pointed at one of the competitors. "Could he have more abs?"

"Oh, here we go." Mitch rolled his eyes. "Do I need to go sit over there?" He pointed to an empty section of bleachers.

"What?" Iris asked. "How can you not be impressed by that?"

"She's right, man," I said. "The dude's lean. Do you think he actually eats?"

"Maybe he should ditch swimming for modeling," Iris threw out.

"What real guy could wear the clothes that he'd wear?" Mitch didn't usually chime in on comments like this. In fact, he usually tuned us out. Iris and I looked at him like he'd mutated. "Don't look at me like that, Theo. We'd never fit in anything he'd wear. Eddie couldn't either."

He was right. Even Eddie with all of his swimmer's sleekness would have a hard time fitting into something this super-thin guy would wear.

"Oh my God, Mitch is arguing over clothes." Iris laughed, and when Mitch didn't take the frown off his face, she strategically attacked his ribs, forcing him to laugh.

He squirmed and tried to move away, but he was sitting on the edge of the row so he didn't have far to go without falling onto the stairs. Iris had mastered the tickle attack. Mitch couldn't move his hands fast enough to keep her away. It was good he wasn't a goalie with those slow reflexes.

"Okay. I'm sorry. You two can ogle all you want, and I'll keep my mouth shut." He relented and she stopped. He scooted back, closer to her.

"You've got nothing to worry about. He's way too thin for me." She ran her hand over his shirt-covered stomach. "And you've got nice abs too." Iris kissed his cheek as a tinge of red flooded over it.

I grinned. They were too cute.

The announcer's voice over the PA got the event

started. There were a few individual events and three relays on the program. Eddie competed in the one-hundred-yard backstroke and anchored one of the relays.

He was poolside getting into his competition mode. During the warm-ups, he was his usual animated self, but once the meet started, he went into his own headspace. A calm fell over his face as he took a seat and put his earbuds in. I asked him once to play for me what he listened to. I expected hard driving music—rock, rap, techno—to get pumped up. But he surprised me with a swelling orchestral score. It reminded me of a medieval knight's movie sound-track. He said it inspired him.

I didn't question it. Athletes have their things they do to get ready to compete. Our goalie listens to the same three Korn songs while he gets dressed. Mitch has to put his gear on in a certain order. I run a specific sequence of warm-ups when I hit the ice.

It was difficult to do anything but watch Eddie. It only took me a few meets before I fell in love with the subtle changes that would come over him as he got himself ready. He'd explained he wanted to be relaxed so he'd be flexible enough to slice through the water like he wanted to.

He sat quietly in his team's area, music on, towel around his bare shoulders and sweatpants on. His eyes were open, but I don't think he really saw what happened around him. He was in Eddie World getting ready to give his best race for the team.

Some of his teammates had their own thing going on, but none of them had intensity like he did.

Once the swimming started, I forced myself to split my attention between Eddie and the pool. Mitch, Iris, and I had our own running commentary on what happened in the races. This meet was important. We were number one and East Boston was number two. The schools had traded rankings most of the season.

"Did Westfield and Northampton actually show up?" Mitch asked. "There's such a gap between East Boston, us, and them. Usually there's decent four-way competition."

"Maybe they know they don't have a chance," Iris said, as usual being the most forthright one in our group.

"Hopelessness sucks," I added. "I've been in games where you know you'll be pummeled. Those aren't fun."

"I'm glad we don't do that anymore." Mitch put his fist out and I bumped it.

He was right. We'd done well our first two seasons at McKinley, and we were holding our own in the rankings this year—in the hunt for a spot to send us to the state playoffs.

"He's on the move." That's what I always said when the towel dropped off Eddie's shoulders. He followed the same pattern every meet—he stood up when the race before his got set, took his earbuds out, wrapped them around a couple of fingers to store them in his sweats pocket, took those off, folded them neatly, and put them on the chair.

I loved his last stretches. He's normally pretty bendy, but these routines were insane. He tried to get me to stretch with him when we worked out together, but I was never flexible like he was.

Mitch reached across Iris and shoved me in the shoulder. "You're about to drool, man. That's even worse than you two all worked up over someone's abs."

"He's doing it over his boyfriend." Iris shoved Mitch like he'd done to me. "Leave him alone."

I pulled myself together. Yes, watching Eddie swim

always horned me up. What was I supposed to do? He was just a few feet away, practically naked, and he looked awesome.

"I bet you don't look like that when you come to one of my games," Mitch added.

"You're not on the ice in super tight swim trunks. Do that, and I'll look exactly like Theo does."

Mitch turned about fifty shades of red before Iris winked at him and turned back to the pool. I grinned, on the verge of laughing. Our banter during the meets was always awesome and silly.

Eddie stepped up to the start point at the same time as his competitors, and they all dropped into the pool. Grabbing on to the handholds in front of him, Eddie waited for the start tone. He pushed off gracefully to arc over the water before dropping in to swim. He had the lead after the start and settled into his stroke, his arms reminding me of windmills as they cut through the water.

"Goooo, Eddie!" I screamed. I was very vocal during his heats. We joked that if he played tennis, I'd get thrown out for making too much noise. Two lanes over, the guy from East Boston pushed hard to catch up. Eddie flipped at the far wall and got a massive push off.

Iris, Mitch, and I all stood up. It was going to be a close one because East Boston worked hard to close the gap. That guy's head was about at Eddie's chest. Eddie's coach yelled something, and Eddie's body pulsed as he added speed at the same time the other guy did. The effort paid off. Eddie touched the wall a fraction of a second before East Boston came in. The race finished in less than a minute.

We cheered and I tried to be extra loud to make up for Eddie's parents not being here.

Eddie looked elated as he came out of the water, pumping his fist in the air a couple of times. He had a huge smile, specifically for winning, and I loved seeing it coming off such a close race. Even the smiles he gave me weren't that big, although they were cuter and sexier. As an athlete I understood.

"He looked really good today," Mitch said.

"Yeah. He's worked hard to improve his time for this week. It paid off."

Eddie finished toweling off and pulled his sweatpants back on. Before he sat to get back in his zone, he looked up in the stands, pointed at me, and winked. That was our thing. He did that after his first swim. I did it when I skated out for the first face-off of the third period.

It took a half hour to get to the final race, the relay. As much as I liked to see Eddie run his own race, watching his team work together for the win and him cranking hard in the anchor spot was the coolest thing of any meet. Watching him extend his team's lead with his powerful strokes or digging deep to make up time needed made me a proud boyfriend.

This relay was the most intense I'd seen this season. East Boston and McKinley were neck and neck the entire way. They had to go to a video to see if Eddie or the other team touched first. Even before they announced, I knew we'd lost because Eddie's face fell.

"I'm gonna head down there," I said. "Catch you guys at Tommy's tonight?"

"Yeah, man." Mitch fist-bumped me.

"Give him a hug for me," Iris said before they left.

I walked down to the edge of the bleachers. I could've gone out onto the deck around the pool, but I never wanted to crowd him or the team. He came over to me once he had his T-shirt and sweats on. We kissed and he rested his forehead against mine. He wasn't usually this upset over losses. Against this school, though, I understood.

"I want to rinse off the chlorine," he said, not moving. "Can you hang a couple minutes?"

"Of course." I gently kissed him.

I sat on the lowest level of seating and watched him head to the locker room with some of his team. Even though, based on points, the team still won the meet, the relay always mattered most to them. I needed to do something special for him tonight to take his mind off it.

My phone pulsed in my pocket, and it was Lorenzo. I wasn't sure he ever took a day off anymore.

"Can you talk?" he asked after he identified.

"Not freely. Let me pop my earbuds in." I looked around, and while no one was near me, this still wasn't a secure location. He could talk, but I'd be careful what I said. I put in my eavesdrop-proof buds. "Go ahead."

"We had a brief lead on the missing file this morning. One of the bots blipped for a couple seconds before going dark again. They must be storing offline and the blip was either a file transfer or, maybe, testing online for something."

"Keeping them offline." I kept my voice low. "It makes sense. Decrypt offline and then use the information when you want. Any idea of location?"

"We couldn't narrow it down any more than to the East Coast."

I sat silent, processing the new information.

"We should vaporize the file the next time we see it." I suddenly envisioned the bots as terminators looking for their target. "Should be doable even within a short time."

"My only fear is that there could be copies we don't

know about. They managed to get it off the laptop. We'd have no way to know if we got them all."

"True. No amount of—" Eddie appeared from the locker room, so I needed to wrap this up. "I gotta go. I'll think on this and get back to you."

"Understood. Later, man."

Crap. Now I had work to do, but I wanted to cheer up Eddie too, preferably before we went to Tommy's.

"Hey," he said, not sounding any better than he looked. "Can I borrow your phone a second? Mine's drained and I need to call Mom back."

"Um. Sure."

I hated letting my phone go, despite the security it had on it. I keyed in the code that would put the phone in super secure mode—none of the TOS stuff would show and no secure calls or messages could come in until it went back into standby.

"Thanks." Eddie took the phone and dialed. "Hey, Mom. Sorry, my phone conked. Yes. I know I should keep it charged better." He rolled his eyes at me. "What's—I planned to hang with Theo."

My watch buzzed and showed the "icing" message. No one I could see in the aquatic center had a phone or computer visible. I also wasn't on Wi-Fi, only standard cell service. I'd have to look and see if Dean was using a different tactic this time.

"But—okay. I'll be home in a few minutes." He clicked off and handed the phone back. "I gotta go home for a few hours. Turns out my grandparents came down to surprise us. Mom's stressed because she doesn't get along with Dad's mother and he's not home."

"S'okay. Still on for tonight?"

"For sure!" He brightened up at that. "We've got plans. I don't care if the grands plan to stay all night."

ELEVEN

I HATED THE MALL, especially on weekend afternoons when everyone else seemed to be there too. I preferred online shopping. The only thing the mall had that I liked was the amazing ice cream place. It had an outside entrance so you didn't have to go inside the rest of the place.

For this trip I ended up deep in the mall, though, because I needed new sneakers and the best place to get those was here. Luckily I knew what I wanted, so I didn't have to stay long. I cut through the food court and I saw Dean at a table with his phone out. He smiled in kind of an evil way and far different from the sullen look I usually saw in school.

It was unsettling.

Part of me wanted to go home since I'd completed my shopping, but Dean and I hadn't talked after he tried to get into my phone. At least no one would pay attention to us if we talked here. His attention seemed to shift between his phone, occasionally tapping the screen, and staring off into the distance. Weird.

Did I do weird stuff like that?

"Hey, Dean." He jumped so hard the table shook. I figured he'd seen me in his peripheral vision so I wouldn't be sneaking up. "Sorry, man. Saw you sitting here and thought I'd say hello."

"What do you want?" I didn't expect the harsh tone or that he'd turn back to where he'd been looking.

I followed his gaze and saw Wes inside The Gap. He was folding pants at a display and had a name tag on his shirt. I didn't take him for the type to have a job, especially in retail. Wes pulled out his phone, looked at it, shook his head, and repocketed it. A few seconds later, he repeated the motion. It reminded me of what he'd done in the parking lot the day Eddie and I pulled him off Dean.

"What are you doing?" I took the chair adjacent to Dean.

"A little revenge."

"You know if he catches you, he'll beat you senseless, right?" Dean's look told me to mind my own business, but I wasn't going to let this go. "Besides, what you're doing is illegal. Tampering with someone's phone."

"Like he'd even figure it out." He didn't look at me. "I vibrate it like it's Gina calling. But when he looks at the screen, there's nothing there. Do you wanna see the pics he's got? His camera roll can be kind of hot sometimes."

I shook my head. Any doubt about who sent the email a couple of days ago disappeared. I snatched the phone out of his hands and kept it out of his reach. At least for the moment, he didn't try to get it back.

"Why not go to the principal and tell her what he's done to you? Eddie and I can be witnesses since we pulled him off you."

"She doesn't care. Wes has been a thorn in my side for years." He held out his hand, but I didn't give him the phone. "Now I can torment him back."

This was not my specialty. I didn't know what to tell him. I was lucky and had limited experience with bullies. Yes, Wes tried to torment me a few years ago. And, in sixth grade some guy wanted my lunch money. I'd said no, he got one punch in, but then I'd wailed on him. I didn't have my TOS training back then, but I still had better reflexes and won easily. While I'd gotten suspended for three days, it set me up as someone not to mess with.

"The school will take action. The athletes all get a big anti-bullying speech at the start of the season."

"Great for you. It doesn't seem to trickle down to goons like him who don't do sports," he said, voice full of sarcasm. He stood and tried to reclaim his phone, but I moved it out of reach too fast. "I'm not like you. Mr. Jock. Mr. MIT. I'm a scrawny guy who wants to be left alone behind a keyboard."

In the store Wes looked at his phone again, frowning as he jabbed at the screen. Dean laughed at Wes's distress.

"Is that why you tried to get into my phone?" I kept his phone, and he dropped back into his chair. "To try to pull this kind of stuff on me?"

He focused on me. "No," he said, some regret in his voice. "Initially I wanted to see if your phone had vulnerabilities like everyone else's. I was curious if the *big-shot cyber expert*," he said as sarcasm took over, "kept himself secure. Once I pinged you and saw the wall you had in place, I wanted to poke it. I didn't expect the meltdown."

I grinned, which seemed to relax him a bit. "Better safe than sorry."

"It's a little extreme for a phone, though, isn't it?" Now

he sounded like the guy at the whiteboard on Friday discussing how the team could design its project. "I mean I've got a firewall up, but you've got extreme security. It's what I'd expect to find on a government or bank server."

"I like to experiment. Good thing I do or who knows what you might try."

"No, man." He sounded sincere. "No way I'd burn you. Why didn't you call me out?"

I shrugged and put his phone on the table between us. "What would've been the point?" This time he shrugged but didn't move for his device. "Here's what I want to know. Why don't you lead the class to get the encryption written for the competition? The team doesn't need me. They've got you."

"I like to stay under the radar. I don't need another reason for the likes of Wes to fuck with me."

In the few minutes I'd sat with him, he'd gone from mad villain to angry to sad.

"Can you show me what you use to protect your phone? I'd love to see that code." The question was a non sequitur.

I pushed back from the table and stood up. "No. What you're doing is so beyond wrong, not to mention Wes could go to the police, and then you'd be in big trouble. There's no way I'm going to show you how to build better defenses when you might try to use it to do something like this, or worse."

He still hadn't touched his phone. He held my gaze and when it was clear he wasn't going to speak, I turned and walked away. I stopped after a few steps and pivoted back.

"If you want me to help you with anything, stop messing with Wes and start stepping up in the team meetings. Be the better man."

I walked away because I wanted him to think about his

response. There was probably a better way to handle him, but it made me angry that people invaded lives like he'd done to Wes. Messing with people's security shouldn't be a game. It's part of why I went into the field as a specialty. Whether I applied my skills for TOS or somewhere else, people deserved to be safe from electronic attacks.

TWELVE

SPINNING around in my desk chair at home, I considered what Dean had done to Wes. He clearly had skills beyond what he showed the team. It left me torn. What Dean was doing was wrong. But in some ways, Wes deserved payback.

And Dean. I'd underestimated him. Being able to trigger the secondary alert on my phone wasn't a simple task. What else did he get into? Was he malicious all the time?

I stopped my spin in front of the keyboard. I hadn't taken the time to look in depth at the logs from my phone yet. With everything going on, it'd been the least of my priorities. But it'd be good insight into Dean to see what his attack looked like.

In short order I'd pulled up my log files and had code spilled across two of my screens. The initial poke on my phone wasn't impressive. Practically any student in the advanced computer-science classes could've done it. The second attack had complexity. Dean had said he only poked the defenses to see what I had, but there was more to this code. If the secondary defense hadn't been in place, he'd have wiped the phone and had all my data.

"No way." I typed at a lightning pace to create a quick script to look for specific patterns in the code. "Holy shit," I muttered.

I'd seen these patterns before. Every sixth line of code was annotated with a specific bit of code that, if displayed in a web browser, would show a lock and key. I wracked my brain to come up with where and why I'd seen this. It'd be so much easier if I could index my brain like Google does the internet.

It had to be TOS related, so I went to the database the IT team kept. We logged information we gathered on cyber security, hackers, and anything else that could possibly be related to keeping the agency tech safe and up-to-date.

What I found shocked me. The annotations were left by a hacker who used the handle Locksmith, or at least that was the nickname they'd been given by the community. It looked like Locksmith never bragged or talked about the hacks performed. Locksmith would get into systems and rearrange a few things. They never left permanent damage, and as far as anyone could determine, never took data. There was always a text file left behind too—*You should really lock that door. You never know who'll come in.*

According to our records, Locksmith had never been apprehended. There were too many other, more serious cases, than someone pointing out an exploit. Consultants were paid to do that all the time. Locksmith seemingly did it for free. If Dean and Locksmith were the same person, he really could be a one-man comp-sci team.

I supposed I was getting ahead of myself. I didn't know for sure if Dean had an alter ego, but the code samples matched what we knew.

Even more confusing was what I should do with this information. Dean knew I had a sample of what he could do, so it wouldn't be beyond belief that I could figure out who he was. I could confront him about Locksmith—or at least that I thought it was him. It wouldn't give anything away about my TOS connection.

What game was he playing with me? There were two other attacks on my gear. Was he responsible for the virus Eddie had on his thumb drive? What about the ping my phone had at Eddie's meet?

I brought up what I'd captured on those two events. I'd cleaned Eddie's computer and thumb drive but kept the data. The virus was sophisticated, designed to aggressively capture all the usernames and passwords from a device. It would've never been caught by store-bought antivirus software. What site would he have visited to end up with that? I reexamined the code and didn't find connections to Locksmith, so I couldn't easily pin that on Dean.

The other attempt on my phone made no sense. The code came through the cell network, as part of the call that couldn't be heard. Eddie had been talking to his mom when it happened. Were Eddie's parents a target and my phone picked up the signal from their side? The signal had a very complex structure, not to mention how it rode along the cell phone signal. This also didn't appear to be from Locksmith. I needed to dig into this code more and see what it was designed to do and why it traveled as part of the audio of a phone call.

I was focused so intently on my screen that I jumped when the chime sounded for an incoming video chat from Lorenzo.

"Winger. Doctor Possible here."

"Hey, Doc."

"You okay?"

"Yeah. The call startled me. I was too invested in a code review."

"Anything interesting?"

"It's weird for sure." I explained the two incidents—Eddie's thumb drive and what happened when Eddie called his mom on my phone. I didn't talk about what I could attribute to Dean because it didn't seem worth the time.

"Do you think someone tried to get to you through Eddie?"

Frankly I hadn't come to that conclusion yet. I'd been considering other options. I let out a long breath. What kind of agent was I if I couldn't see the obvious?

"Don't beat yourself up. You're still putting pieces together. However, it's the first thing I thought of. Since the tracker mission, you don't exactly live in a bubble anymore. People saw you and know what you can do. If they've put together that you and Eddie are a couple, they might use that to get more intel."

I sat back in my chair. I desperately wanted to spin around, but that seemed rude since Lorenzo was on the screen. "Do you think he's in danger?"

"It's just a theory. There's no concrete evidence. His thumb drive could have been compromised in so many ways via public networks. The phone's a little more difficult to figure out. He'd have to call the person who would send the signal, unless someone hijacked the call. I might be reading more into it than there is."

I didn't feel much better. "I'll log the code snippets into the database. Can you assign it out to be analyzed for any known characteristics?"

"Sure. Let me know when it's there and I'll make it a priority."

"Thanks. Now, what can I do for you?"

"Wanted to run something by you to see if you think it's viable."

"Of course. Tell me."

"You know how when you delete a file from a computer it's not really gone until you rewrite or reformat the space it occupied? Could we send bots out to look for where the file might've been? We've tried to find the actual file, which hasn't worked because it seems they're keeping it off the internet as much as possible. What if we looked for artifacts that might give us some direction?"

"Interesting idea, and theoretically it should work. The bots would have to be able to scan drives on that level. It'd be a riff on data recovery software." I paused to think for a moment. "What I'd worry about is the bot staying stealth. When we're in systems and looking at the regular directories, it doesn't take much time. For this to work, though, we'd have to be there long enough to read the data that's not in the directory anymore. Depending on the security, it might raise an alert. On the other hand, we don't have much to lose. As per usual, the bot can self-destruct if any alarms are tripped."

Lorenzo nodded and typed on the keyboard in front of him. "Yeah, I'm worried about the time it would take to scan any deleted files, especially analyzing data fragments."

"I'd have it do fragments last. I'd recommend three tiers of scanning—regular file directories, deleted files that are intact, and then fragments. I imagine it'll take us some time to be able to accurately look for remnants. Maybe deploy bots with the first two while we develop the third."

"I'll take a first pass on writing this thing." Lorenzo seemed excited for the first time in several days. "Will you review it once I've got it?"

"For sure."

His expression took a somber turn. "We're having a wake for Keys on Thursday at HQ. If you want to come, I've arranged a private plane to bring you and a car to get you from the airport. It's up to you. I know a weekday evening isn't the best for you."

"Let me talk to my dad. If he's okay with it, I'll make it work. I want to be there."

Lorenzo nodded. "Let me know." He paused for a moment. "I'm going to get to work and I'll let you know how it goes. I'll update you on the code you're sending over too. Later." The screen went dark.

I finally spun around in the chair, speeding up with each pass. There was so much to distill out of that conversation. Not only a new bot idea to churn over, but the idea that someone might be using Eddie. I stopped the spin cycle so I could upload the files to the database. There was still Dean to figure out too.

Once the data transfer completed, I shoved all of it aside because I had tests to study for.

THIRTEEN

"We're still on for tonight, right?" Eddie asked as I leaned against the lockers next to his. The computer-science team was meeting daily this week leading into this weekend's competition. Eddie's locker had become our end-of-day meeting point before he headed out.

"Yes we are!" A weekday date night called for extra excitement.

We didn't usually go out on school nights because of our packed schedules. We made exceptions for special events, though. Tonight we were headed to Boston University where Barry Jenkins would be interviewed and take audience questions.

We'd been moved by his movie *Moonlight*. Beyond the interview, several shorts were going to be screened and discussed. Eddie and I freaked out when the school announced the event because in person would be better than any DVD commentary. The tickets were not easy to get. I ended up helping two graduate film students put together a massive computer system to do their editing and CGI on. It was worth it, though.

"I'll pick you up?" Eddie had turned seventeen in December, so he could finally drive us instead of taking separate cars.

"That works. I'm headed home after the team meeting so I'll be there by five."

"See you at six, then." Eddie gave me a quick peck and headed off to swim practice.

I walked quickly to the classroom so I wasn't late. I had to snag Dean today too. He'd avoided me the past couple of days—he'd come into meetings late and dashed out before I could catch him. I had just the trick to get his attention.

"Whoa!" As I walked past the restroom, the door opened and instead of someone coming out I got pulled inside.

Wes, of course. And a couple of his goons too.

"What the fuck, Wes?"

"I still owe you, Reese. I'm flunking math, and you posted all the stuff about me."

He thought I was messing with him? Great.

I sized up the situation and this wasn't really a problem. My skills should let me take on these three.

"I *saw* that stuff like everyone else. I didn't send any of it."

"Do you think I'm stupid?" His loud voice echoed throughout the tiled restroom. "You're the only one smart enough to do that." He stepped into my personal space. Close enough I could smell that he hadn't showered after P.E. "You're gonna fix my phone and do my homework."

"I haven't done anything to your phone." I held my ground. "And I'm not doing your homework."

My unzipped hoodie gave him an easy way to grab on and pull me closer. "Oh, you'll do it, or we'll break you.

Your boy's not here to back you up and neither are your teammates."

Time to end this.

Apparently he hadn't listened when *I* said I'd break his arm. His goons flanked him, so I had one good move to make on Wes before they'd get involved.

I felt a little bad for my response, but I knew it'd be effective and free me from his grip. I thrust my knee into his balls. I hadn't learned that from John or Coach, but its effectiveness couldn't be disputed. Sure enough he released me and dropped to the floor while an impressive list of mangled curse words flew out of his mouth.

His crew moved in. I had some space, so I kicked out and nailed one in the chest. He went off-balance and careened into a stall door and then fell in. The other guy got too close and connected a punch to my ribs, which landed with enough impact to knock me back a couple of steps.

"Get him!" Wes directed from the ground where he was cupping his junk. The one that had gone into a stall still thrashed around on the floor. The other guy seemed determined to try to box, which was silly. The more he moved, the more I saw his patterns. It made it easy to weave out of the way, grab his wrist, and pivot him so I had his arm behind his back.

He cussed now too.

"Are we done?" I asked as his friend emerged from the stall. He stayed back and leaned against the door.

The more the guy I held struggled, the more pressure I put on his arm. "No way," he grunted.

"Okay."

I shoved my foot just below his knee cap, which took his leg out from under him. I pushed him away, and he tumbled to the floor.

"What's going on in here?" I turned to find Mitch in the doorway. With the scene in front of him, the look of surprise on his face was justified. "Theo?"

"Wes and his goons ambushed me." I moved to Mitch's side, while keeping watch on the trio.

"I'm gonna get you so bad, Reese." It was hard to take Wes seriously since he struggled to get to his feet, still clearly in pain while his guys were also sidelined. The guy at the stall didn't even help out his friend who gripped the back of his leg, trying to massage the pain away.

I moved to stand over Wes, and Mitch stayed close. He knew how to back me up without even a word. "You'll do nothing. If I hear that you mess with anyone else, or that your friends do, I won't come after you. I'll see to it the school does. I'm not afraid to report you."

I turned and walked out without another word, and Mitch followed.

"Who are you?" he asked, laughing a little while we walked down the hall. "Did you take all three?"

I shrugged and tried to play it off, even though I was happy with myself. "Hockey players don't take shit."

"Yeah, man." Out of the corner of my eye, I saw Mitch watch me as he tried to figure out how I managed a three-on-one. "You worried they'll tell Ms. Cohen?"

"No way. They won't go to the principal. They'd have to admit they couldn't handle one person. Besides, if they do, I'll tell my side of the story, that they ambushed me."

"And with your awesome rep, she'll take your word for sure. Where're you headed?"

"Comp-sci team."

"Oh yeah. There's a pickup game at Porazzo. Drop by after if you want."

"No can do. Date night."

"All right, see you at practice, then."

We stopped outside the classroom. "Catch you later."

We fist-bumped and I went inside. The team clustered around screens, already at work. Mrs. H gave me a look that asked where I'd been. I wouldn't be sent to detention since we were after school hours, but her gaze made it clear she didn't like late.

"Sorry," I said quietly, coming up to her desk. "I got caught up with something."

She shifted her expression to a slight smile. It was probably a reflex to give late comers an evil eye. "The team came in and got right to work on their entry."

"Great," I said as I stood next to her desk. "What do you think? Let them work until we're down to half an hour and then review?"

"Sounds good, unless you guys decide we need to do something different."

I nodded at her and then went to the cluster of students to let them know the plan. They barely acknowledged me. I recognized the look on their faces—they were in the zone.

I took a seat in my usual spot and went to work on my plan to get Dean's attention. I pulled up a list of phones that were in the room, and they were easy to identify with some aspect of the student's name in the ID. Dean, however, named his phone "Not Yours." He had some nice security, and I tested it before deciding how I'd breach it. In a few minutes, I'd finished.

I made his phone vibrate in a repeating pattern of three quick pulses and three seconds of silence. When it didn't stop after a few cycles, he took it from his jeans pocket. I'd placed a message on the screen that read *We need to talk. Your phone is locked until we do.*

Dean didn't even look at me. He pocketed the phone and continued to work with the team.

There were a couple of questions while they worked. When it came time to review, Jessie and Dean presented on the big screen.

They'd made a lot of progress in the past two days. It looked like Dean had taken my advice to lead them more. The entry was more advanced, but not so much it didn't look like it belonged to the team. There were fewer obvious weaknesses to exploit so they were on the right track.

"This looks really good guys."

"There's a *but* in there, I can hear it," Jessie said while she and Dean were still at the front of the class.

"I'm gonna sound like a dick saying it this way—"

"Theo, this may be after school...."

Oops. I shouldn't have said that in this setting. "Sorry, Mrs. H." I looked to her apologetically before returning to the team. "I see places I could get in, but I'm not sure your competitors would find them."

I left it there to get their reaction.

Dean spoke up. "What if you told us the areas to look at but didn't tell us more than that? See if we can fix it."

"Let's do it." I went over the four things that were the most concerning, in order from most to least exploitable. There were more, but I didn't think most high schoolers would see them. I told them there were more, but to focus on these since the competition was just three days away.

"Cool. Thanks, Theo." Jessie smiled and returned to her desk. Dean followed.

"One more order of business we need to consider," said Mrs. H, coming over to the team. "We need to appoint co-captains, who will represent the team to the officials. I'd like for you all to decide who that is by the time we meet tomorrow. We have to declare the captains at the same time we upload our entry Friday morning."

That set the group buzzing. I stayed out of it and looked over the entry again to make sure I hadn't missed anything. It would take me longer than five minutes to get into this, and that made me proud.

"Can Theo be one of the captains?" Alice asked.

"He is a registered member of the team, so he could."

"I don't think that's fair to you guys." I looked first at Mrs. H and then the team. "This is your work. Making me a captain gives me way too much credit."

"But you've helped a lot." Alice pushed for her suggestion.

"Who do you think should be captains?" Jessie asked.

I didn't want to play favorites, but I definitely had an opinion. "I'm not sure my vote should count either."

"Sure it does. Mrs. H said you were part of the team."

"My vote would go for you and Dean."

"Told you," Li said. "Exactly the suggestion I made."

They went back to their debate. They didn't ask me anything else, so I stood by. After a few minutes, Mrs. H called an end to the day's meeting.

Everyone left quickly, except Dean, who scowled at me from his desk. I packed up my laptop and jerked my head toward the door so he'd follow.

"See you tomorrow, Mrs. H," I called as I left.

"Have a good afternoon, Theo."

Dean wasted no time once we were a few steps from the classroom in the empty hall. "Locking my phone, really?"

"It got your attention," I said, keeping my voice low while we walked side by side. "And we need to talk."

"I told you I wasn't going to try to break your security again, what's the—"

"I analyzed your hacks and I saw something familiar. You're Locksmith."

Dean stopped, and I turned to face him. Color drained from his face, and I thought for a moment he might pass out. "I don't know what you're talking about." His voice became monotone.

He started walking again, faster. I had no trouble keeping up.

"Yeah, you do." I grabbed him by the shoulder and forced him to stop. "That's why you can attack my phone, and why you can send out email like it's from Wes. It's also why you're so valuable to the team."

"I told you, I don't want that kind of visibility." He tried to shrug me off.

"Look, I'm not going to tell anyone that you're Locksmith. I know you never stole anything. Frankly I think you should consider going into security."

"Like you?"

"You've got the skills."

"You make it sound like I could start tomorrow."

"It's not that easy, but once you're in college, there'll be plenty of internship opportunities."

He snorted a laugh. "College. Right. I don't catch the breaks you do."

"Have you talked to anyone? Mrs. Robbins or Mrs. H?"

"Mrs. Robbins only wants to help people she can get placed. My grades are shit, except for Mrs. H and math because there's nothing I can't handle there. And I gotta help—"

We stared at each other for a few moments. "Help what?" I finally asked.

"Nothing." He pulled his jacket tighter around him. "Just leave it. I gotta go. Unlock my phone or don't. I don't care." He spun on his heel and headed back the way we'd come.

I let him go. There was more to Dean than I'd first guessed. Could I even help if he told me the problem? He certainly wouldn't tell me anything while he was angry. I pulled my phone out and sent the unlock command.

I headed for the school office. If Ms. Cohen was still there, I'd solve one problem—Wes.

FOURTEEN

THE DIRECTOR's talk was incredible. He discussed the making of *Moonlight* and screened some of his earlier work. We'd been to a couple of programs like this before, but this one went above and beyond because he stayed to talk with the audience after the official program had ended.

"I can't believe we got to see that." Eddie slipped his hand into mine as we exited into the chilly evening.

"I loved it."

"Sometimes I forget the perks of dating a college boy." He squeezed my hand as we headed for the car and I squeezed back.

"Can we walk for a little bit?"

"Sure."

We went past where he'd parked, and after a while in silence, I finally decided to tell him what I'd done. "I reported Wes Lockly after the comp-sci meeting."

Eddie turned his head and raised his eyebrow. "That's a surprise. Did something happen?"

I hadn't gone into this before our date because I didn't want him distracted during the show. I laid out everything, although I tried to underplay my takedown of the three. There were no lies, though, because I didn't want any awkward moments if he discussed any of this with Mitch.

"I wasn't going to say anything, but then I decided I had to because it might put a stop to it." I left a pause for him to respond. When he didn't I continued. "I mean we should've told Ms. Cohen when we caught him wailing on Dean. At least this time, I can bear the brunt of any fallout without involving Dean or you. At least I hope so."

He, somewhat awkwardly, kissed my cheek while we walked. "As if you don't have enough going on already, you take up the cause to stop the school bully. Do you actually sleep at some point?"

I raised his hand to my mouth and kissed his knuckles. "I had to say something. If he's willing to take on a jock, who knows what he does to some of the students who can't defend themselves."

"Well, if you need me to say anything, I'll do it."

"I know."

After a few quiet moments, Eddie looked at me. "Seems like you want to say more."

He had no idea. I decided, for once, that I'd talk. "Remember I told you about the woman I worked with that died?" I took a deep breath. "Sometimes it's... I don't know... it's surreal. I don't always know what to think about it. I'm going to her wake tomorrow night. I've never been to a wake and...." I sighed. What else was there to say?

Eddie stopped us, forcing people to go around before he gently pulled me toward the grassy area that ran next to the sidewalk. He wrapped me in a hug and kissed the top of my head. He simply held me. It felt good. Even more, it felt safe.

"Is there anything I can do?" he finally asked.

"Honestly, the hug has been pretty good."

"You can have those anytime." He kissed my head again and I stepped back, keeping one of his hands in mine so we could walk again. "I'm glad you told me. Do you want company for the wake?"

"I wish I could. It's a private thing."

He nodded and we got back to our walk. "You guys ready for the competition this weekend?" Eddie shifted topics at the right time.

"I think so. I really liked what the team had today. They've paid attention to what I told them and it showed."

"Is there something I can come watch on Sunday? See you guys take the championship?"

"I actually don't know." It occurred to me that, other than the competition happening on the Amherst College campus, and that it went for thirty hours straight, I was kind of clueless. "Why would you want to watch a bunch of people sitting around computers anyway?"

"Because you're one of them, silly. I like the look you get when you're thinking super hard."

"You're weird." He stuck his tongue out at me and I smirked back. "I'll see what the deal is. Be cool to see you and make silly faces at you that'll confuse everyone else."

The team planned to leave for Amherst Friday afternoon to settle in and be ready for Saturday morning. Since I had a game Friday night, I'd catch up with them around midnight.

"Maybe I should come with you Friday and we can share a room. That was awesome in Denver." Eddie grinned and wiggled his eyebrows at me. He was ridiculously cute and it made my insides tingle in the best way.

While a lot of bad stuff had gone down in Denver, spending alone time with Eddie always made me happy.

It'd said a lot about him that he didn't get too weird when things got super chaotic. I suspected most people would've run from the mess, but he stayed right there.

"Unfortunately I'll have roommates Friday. And once we start Saturday morning, we go straight through into Sunday afternoon."

"If I can get there on Sunday, maybe we could make the trip back together?"

"That would rock. Dad and I were already debating the best way for me to get there. If he drives me up, maybe you could bring me back. We'll figure it out."

"You really got into doing this thing, didn't you?"

I cocked my head and looked at him, trying to figure out what he meant.

"Coaching the team," he coaxed.

"I've enjoyed it more than I thought I would. And I didn't give them the credit they deserve."

"I figured you'd end up liking it."

"Why?"

"You like helping people. I can tell it when you help me with a computer thing, or if you're explaining something. There's never a condescending tone that you know more than someone else."

"I think the team would disagree with that," I said, kicking a pebble along in front of me. "I'm not always as modest as I should be."

"But I bet you're usually happy to give them the information. I bet you'll be a teacher someday."

"Nah. I like doing the actual work too much."

"Lots of people teach and work."

"What about you? Mr. Getting Me Through Science Class."

"It's possible. Maybe college level one day."

"I can totally see you as the sexy teacher everyone wants. You'll teach a few days a week and cure diseases the rest of the time."

"That's me—Doctor Teacher."

We chuckled. We knew what our basic futures looked like—me continuing to study cyber security at MIT and Eddie in biochemistry at UMass Boston. But we rarely talked about what might come next.

We tended to be practical. We knew the odds of still being together in four or five years were not exactly in our favor. We'd had that talk once, shortly after we started going out and we got our first SAT scores back—we've already got a date planned in the spring for us to retake them, so the topic might come up again. Even though we planned to go to college in the same city, we knew we couldn't predict everything that could happen in the year and a half before we graduated high school much less when we got to college. We might be a love that starts in high school and runs forever, but we could also find that college pulls us in different directions.

"What do you want to do for your birthday?" The topic change came out of nowhere. "We've got that double cele-bration in a few weeks."

Wow. There were less than three weeks before Valentine's and another ten days before I'd turn seventeen. Eddie almost never planned in advance. That usually fell to me.

"I hadn't really thought about it yet." Eddie'd been super sweet last year—the first birthday/Valentine's combo we'd celebrated together. He'd treated me to pizza and cupcakes. It'd been very sweet because he orchestrated everything. He even asked my parents if I could go out on my birthday, just in case they'd planned something.

"Can I put it together again?"

"Hell yeah!" I said, perhaps too loud because the couple walking in front of us turned to stare. We looked at each other and laughed quietly.

"What'd you have in mind?" I asked.

He made a face that I caught out of the corner of my eye. "You don't get to know."

I made my best disappointed expression. "Okay," I said, sounding disappointed even as I broke into a smile. "I look forward to it."

"Cool." Eddie looked at his watch. "I suppose we should get you home. Don't want your coach mad at me for keeping you out too late."

We had a leisurely walk to the car. I knew I'd be fine for practice in the morning if for no other reason than this evening was so perfect.

FIFTEEN

It'd been a long time since I'd shown up for practice early. As I'd gotten busier, I'd stopped doing something I truly enjoyed. But now bike rides weren't doing the trick anymore to let me relax and clear my head, I hoped time on the ice would bring me some clarity.

It'd felt good talking with Eddie about some things last night. The talk, however, only added to the list that demanded processing time in my already overworked brain. That talk made me so happy, though.

Across the center line, there were pucks ready to go. I sprinted from one end of the rink, picked up a puck, and drove in on the empty net. Approaching the net, I'd decide where I wanted to hit. To make it challenging, I aimed the shots to ping off a post and land behind the goal line. The game was not only fun, it helped improve my shooting accuracy.

I loved the sounds of being the only person on the ice— my skates scraping the surface, the pop of the puck on my stick, the pings off the posts. Perhaps more than wheels on the road and the wind whipping around me, these were Zen moments.

Keys and the job offer filled my thoughts while my skating went on autopilot. I still paid attention to my shots even while I mulled over what to do. Keys was the first person I've worked with who'd died. It's possible agents I had assisted on missions have been killed in the line of duty, but it didn't happen while I worked with them. The way TOS was set up, I didn't have routine contact with agents I'd worked with. My parents were the exception to that. Field agents were dispersed around the world, and for security purposes, no one had access to the full agent list. Security around that only increased after the tracker breach last year.

The only people I knew well worked in IT because we were a team that constantly worked together. We also weren't in the line of fire often. After the Denver trip last year, I'd talked more to Lorenzo because I wanted to know about his field experience. While he traveled a few times a year, he was usually only in close proximity to make the work easier, exactly like he'd been with me on the tracker mission. He'd never been the primary agent like I'd ended up being.

What I didn't know, and might never, is why Keys went on the mission. If I'd been able to get in and make it seem like Cocoon had finished the job, why couldn't Keys have worked from afar with another agent in the chair? It wasn't that I wished someone else dead in Keys's place, but a trained field agent might have managed the situation better, and maybe no one would've been killed.

Did Keys go by choice or was she ordered to go? I'd gone by choice. It was the only solution I'd seen, because Dad's life was on the line, and maybe Mom's too. Would I eventually be ordered to go somewhere too and possibly end up like Keys? Could I do that?

My speed on the ice picked up. I got a puck on my stick. I wasn't sure I could go fast enough to help me figure out the answers. Driving toward the net, I shot from the top of the slot and got the clank as I watched the puck drop from the top right corner to behind the line. Going around the net, I picked up one of the pucks I'd shot and missed with. Sprinting hard toward center ice, I bypassed the rubber disks there and kept what I had. As I crossed the blue line, I unleashed an anguished cry at the same time I sent a slap shot toward the net.

The shot caused a loud thud off the boards since I aimed wide of the goal.

Where had the scream come from? I didn't feel a melt-down was imminent like on the bridge. Why the howl? Luckily no one was around. I'd talk to Shields about it in case I was losing my mind or something.

I dug my skates into the ice, coming to a hard stop near the puck.

Maybe I needed to approach Lorenzo's offer like I did a decryption scenario.

There were facts that I knew.

Keys had more experience than I do.

I'm very good at my current job, maybe better than anyone else currently at TOS. Lorenzo seemed to think I met that criteria.

Working with a team, even leading one, I could do. I'd been on teams for years, and now I coached one and seemed to be doing okay.

Could I truly manage people in their jobs, though? Ones who would be older, sometimes much older, than me? I had no idea.

I pulled a puck toward me with the stick blade and took off toward the other end of the rink.

What if I sent someone to their death? Did Lorenzo know that's what he was doing with Keys, or had Keys put herself in that position?

Crossing the far blue line, I didn't curve in to the net, choosing to stay along the boards. Making the turn behind the net, I wanted to move the puck and skate fast.

It was possible I was overthinking. I tended to do that when there wasn't a logical conclusion to be reached. As far as I knew, Keys was the first from IT to be killed in the line of duty.

I charged up the other side of the ice, pushing like I had an entire team chasing me. My legs had a good burn happening. This time as I crossed the blue line, I made for the net and I made the pipe at the far left my target. I made a hard stop at the top of the circle and fired. The clank was very satisfying.

Three hard taps on the glass startled me.

"Hey!"

It was Mitch.

We both headed for the rink door.

"Damn, man, you're early," he said, opening the door from the outside.

"Yeah." I peeled off my helmet and wiped my sleeve across my face to make sure sweat didn't drip into my eyes.

"And you've apparently been at it for a while. You're gonna have something left in the tank for the actual practice, I hope."

"For sure." I stole a look at the scoreboard clock, and Mitch was about thirty minutes early too. "What about you? You usually get here with just enough time to hit the ice."

"Wanted to sharpen my skates, but that can wait. You want some company?"

Mitch and I going one-on-one would be a blast from the past.

"For sure."

Mitch's face lit up far more than expected. "Five minutes." He jogged off to the locker room.

I slowly skated over to the bench, picking up a puck along the way to move with my skates as if I played soccer rather than hockey. Once there I grabbed my Gatorade and took a long drink. The cold beverage was delicious after so much skating. After the drink, I toweled my head off again and took a moment to breathe.

Storing the towel next to my drink, I slipped my helmet back on and lined up a bunch of pucks at the top of the slot. I proceeded to rapidly aim and fire slap shots toward the net. Every clank made me happy since this was all about rapidly hitting any metal around the net. About 75 percent seemed to hit where I wanted.

Mitch charged onto the ice with his water bottle and quickly dropped it onto the bench.

"Okay, what are we playing?"

"Keep away." I knocked a puck over to him.

"You're on."

He skated backward, away from me, and took the puck with him on his stick and sometimes on his skate blades. The idea was simple—don't give up the puck to the other person. This was one of my favorite games. We'd learned it as a one-on-one drill years ago, and it remained one of my favorite things to do. It was like solving a security problem— you had to look for patterns and weaknesses to exploit.

Playing with Mitch was a blast. Sadly it was only about fifteen minutes before others showed up on the ice. We kept going, dodging around our teammates for an extra challenge.

"That was awesome," Mitch said when we stopped at the bench.

"Yeah. You're even better than I remember."

"And you've become the poke-check king. You should play more defense with that skill." Mitch took a long drink while the coaches approached the ice.

"We should do this more often."

"Yeah, man. Anytime you wanna come in early, let me know."

We hadn't done this since summer camp because of our schedules. Or, more truthfully, mine. This is what Dad wanted me to see—the importance of taking the time to be with friends.

"Monday? Once I'm back from the competition."

"I'm there." He grinned and I did too.

While I didn't have answers yet about taking the promotion, I did have some clarity. My schedule needed an overhaul so there would be more time for Eddie and my friends.

SIXTEEN

Dad picked me up from school before the end of classes and took me to one of the small airfields outside of town. I got on a private plane and flew for ninety minutes to an airfield outside Richmond, Virginia, where a car picked me up and whisked me to TOS HQ.

On the plane I'd changed from my sweatshirt to a button-up shirt, tie, and jacket. I kept the jeans and sneakers. I hated dressing up, but Keys's wake deserved more than a sweatshirt. Dad didn't even have to talk me into it. I'd packed it on my own.

This was our chance to say our goodbyes because none of us could go to the actual funeral. Joanna would go as part of Keys's cover story that she worked in IT security for a large financial institution. The emotions ran high in the large conference room everyone was gathered in. I felt better knowing I wasn't the only one all over the place with my feelings.

I didn't see Lorenzo when I entered the room. I gave a quick wave to Ram and Pascale, two techs I often worked with on gadget projects. I recognized some people from my internship, but there were many new faces, though I probably knew them by codename since emails zipped back and forth all the time.

"Winger, it's great to meet you in person finally." I turned to find a woman who looked to be about my mom's age. "I'm Pyramid."

"Oh my God. It's awesome to meet you too." I extended my hand and she shook it, but she then pulled me into a gentle hug. She worked in the security division and cataloged the vast amounts of information we took in to make sure it stayed organized. "You can call me Theo."

"Pamela. I'm sorry it took this for us to finally meet. But it's great to put a face to all the emails."

A lot of work happened via email or voice chat, so we didn't often see each other. Lorenzo was one of the few people I used video to communicate with. On official channels we always used codenames too, to help maintain security.

"You too." I looked around the room. "It's great there are so many people here. Keys deserves it."

"Yes she does. She was always great to work with. Even in the most serious situations, she came across as calm, and the team needed that stability."

Emotions swallowed my ability to respond. In a motherly moment, she put her arm around my shoulder. "In the past couple of months, I'd worked with her almost as much as Lorenzo since we'd updated all the security protocols." My voice cracked in the middle of the sentence.

"It's okay." She must've seen the frown on my face. "Most everyone's a mess in here."

"Theo, so glad you're here." Lorenzo pulled me into a bear hug.

"Good to see you." We released our embrace, and he

stood next to me. Pamela, meanwhile, simply gave me a nod and stepped away. "How are you?"

"I honestly didn't know how many people would be able to get here for this. You know, pulling together a bunch of secret agents isn't the easiest thing to do." He smiled weakly and I nodded. "Some people came from Europe. One tried to get here from China, but the connection in Denver was delayed."

"Keys worked with a lot of people. I'm not surprised at all."

"There are great stories circulating too."

"I bet. She had a cracked sense of humor, and her sense of timing was incredible."

"Oh my God, yes." Lorenzo smiled while his eyes betrayed his sadness. "Listen, can I grab you for a few minutes in private?"

"Of course."

Joanna cut us off when we headed for the door. "Theo. Always good to have you here, although I'm sorry it's for this."

"I'm glad I could make it." We shook hands.

"Are you two going to be gone long?"

"Shouldn't be more than a few minutes," Lorenzo answered for us.

Joanna's nod and expression implied that she knew what Lorenzo had on his agenda. I wasn't surprised by that since she was in charge.

We walked and ended up at Lorenzo's office. He'd increased the number of action figures on the shelves over his desk considerably from last summer. I wanted to check them out up close, but this wasn't the time.

"I'm curious if you'd made a decision yet." Lorenzo dropped into his desk chair, and I took the one across from him. "If you need more time, it's okay. But since you're here, it seemed it was a good time to talk."

I took a deep breath. I knew my answer, but I was suddenly nervous to give it. I'd planned to tell Lorenzo at the end of the evening. He just beat me to the punch.

"I've thought a lot about it. From a technical standpoint I say yes. I can certainly review the team's work, offer guidance, and take responsibility for the decisions TOS makes on security."

He nodded. "I'm glad you'll take the technical duties. We'll craft the job so that's all it is. You'll still manage teams on tech projects. I'll handle mission assignments and other management details."

I'm glad he took it well. He was the last person at TOS I wanted to disappoint.

"I'll take on more in the summer, and once I'm in college we'll figure out what that means. Provided you and Joanna still want me."

"You're taking on plenty. Believe me. And we'll bolster the security team too so there's more people with the skills you and Keys have." A ripple of emotion flowed through me when he didn't use the past tense for Keys. "We shouldn't have been caught like we were. We'll have a meeting every month to determine if we need to change our approach. I know you and I talk all the time anyway, but we should set aside time to specifically discuss how you're handling the responsibilities."

I tried, and failed, to suppress a laugh.

"What?" he asked, smiling. At least I hadn't offended him with what slipped out.

"You sounded so much like a boss."

He snickered. "Yeah, that doesn't happen much. I guess

it's good I can do that in case I ever need to get some other kind of job."

It was one of those weird oddities of working for TOS, because I didn't usually feel like I had a boss so much as a collaborator. Sure I knew how real jobs worked. Mitch worked at a sporting goods store. Eddie had lifeguard duty at an indoor pool. I heard stories about how managers were. TOS had a human resources department, because there were basics like paying people and making sure taxes and health insurance were taken care of. But Lorenzo rarely seemed like a boss to me.

"I'd like to announce it to the team on Monday," Lorenzo said. "Is that okay? I was thinking a video conference so we could all see each other."

I considered. It seemed fast but someone needed to take up the responsibilities. Nerves made my insides quivery—reminding me how it felt to be a kid and knowing you've done something wrong and you were just waiting to get caught.

"Monday's good. That'll put the computer-science competition behind me, and I can work on getting up to speed on everything Keys worked on."

"You won't have to catch up overnight, you know," Lorenzo said with a slight smile. "There's time. And we've got plenty of documentation on what the most critical projects are so you'll know where to focus. And Joanna and I will fully support you."

I knew he'd never let me down. I smiled at him. "Thanks. I'll do my best."

"I know." He stood up and so did I. He threw an arm around my shoulder but stopped me before he opened the door. "By the way, you didn't ask, but this comes with a 32 percent pay increase."

I forced my mouth to stay closed because my initial reaction was for it to hit the floor. I already made a ton of money. Despite my age, they paid me like I was a regular employee. They'd made the decision two years ago to pay me a full-time salary to match the workload.

Mom and Dad, early on, set me up with a good savings plan. I took an allowance that we agreed on, and I could access money for large purchases—like new computers—if I needed to. My savings were about to grow in a staggering way.

"Cool." I didn't know what else to say.

Lorenzo looked at his watch. "We should get back to everyone."

As we walked in, people were telling stories about Keys. I had a couple I wanted to tell, even though the thought of it made me skittish because I wanted to do right by her. I listened to a few stories and then stepped up to tell my own about Keys teaching me about encryption and music. At the end, I raised my glass of ginger ale in salute.

Over the next couple of hours, I put a lot of codenames to faces. Another good reason for me to be here before the changes were announced.

By the time I headed back to the airport, I was tired but very glad I said my goodbyes to a colleague and mentor.

SEVENTEEN

"That was a great game," Dad said as I dropped into a chair across from him and next to Eddie. They'd been waiting for me in the rink lobby, waiting for me to change out of my gear. "It's been too long. I hope I didn't bore Eddie too much with my constant chatter on how awesome you were."

"That's never boring." Eddie grabbed my hand from the tabletop. "Theo is awesome."

"It hasn't been that long since you've been here. You saw one at the beginning of December, before the holiday break."

"I know. I like watching you play, though. I wonder how I ended up with such an athletic son."

"What do you mean?" I made a face. "You played basketball."

"I only played because they needed someone else tall. I'd never call myself a basketball player." He looked at his watch. "Shall we hit the road?"

"Yeah. Can we stop somewhere and pick up a burger along the way? I'm hungry."

"Of course."

Eddie and Dad stood up, and I took that chance to hug Eddie. "I'll see you Sunday night."

"Yup. Keep me posted on how the competition goes?"

"We can't have phones or our own computers in the competition rooms. But I'll text on breaks."

"Cool. Go get another win." He leaned in for a kiss that I might've been a little too happy to receive. At least Dad didn't say anything about the PDA, even though there were a couple of cat calls from my teammates as they passed.

Eddie and I chuckled when we broke the kiss.

"They're just jealous because they don't have someone to kiss them in the lobby." I gave Eddie another quick kiss.

We three walked out of the rink together, and at Dad's car I hugged Eddie again.

"See you in a couple days." I hugged Eddie again.

"Don't let him totally geek out, Mr. Reese."

I looked at both of them and rolled my eyes.

"I'll do my best. Good night, Eddie."

One more kiss and then Eddie headed toward his Jeep, and Dad and I were on our own.

"You know, you didn't have to drive me to Amherst. I could've taken Mom's car since she's gone."

"I know. But this is my chance to be a dad for a while. I don't get to do that enough. That's okay, right? I'm not doing—"

"It's completely okay. I wanted to make sure you knew you didn't have to."

I enjoyed hanging out with Dad, so it was cool he'd decided to drive. Whether it was watching TV, having him at a game, or taking a mini-road-trip, I appreciated the time with him. I even thought it was cool he planned to stay in Amherst for the weekend. There was nothing to *see* since we were to be sequestered for a day and a half in a classroom. There would be an awards ceremony and reception Sunday afternoon, but that was it. Eddie and I decided he shouldn't make the trip for that since he wouldn't be able to see me compete.

Once we were in the car and heading out of the parking lot, I asked Dad, "Have you decided what you're going to do while I'm with the team?"

"Saturday I thought I might go see a movie. There's a theater near the hotel, and the new *Star Wars* is there." He sounded excited, like it might be a minivacation for him. "I haven't been to the movies in a long time, and a blast from the past seemed a good way to spend some time."

"You'll like it. It's really good."

"You've seen it?"

"Eddie and I went a couple weeks ago after a game."

"Anyway, for sure that. There's an indoor pool too, so I may hang out and read."

"Good to know you've got plans."

Once we got outside the city, we found an exit with a Dairy Queen, where I got a bacon cheeseburger, a chocolate shake, and fries. Dad and I split the fries, so I left them in the console between the seats. After eating, we settled in for the drive while eighties songs played on the satellite radio. He and Mom tended to go back and forth between the eighties and nineties on trips. I enjoyed that music far more than his other preferred genre, metal, which I didn't understand.

"Can I ask how last night was?" he asked after we'd been quiet a while.

"It was good. I'm glad I went since a lot of people came. There were some amazing stories told about Keys, and I'm glad I got to hear them. She clearly had an impact on people. Meeting some of the IT team that works outside of HQ was great too. Emails, voice chat, and codenames are good, but I liked talking in person."

Dad sighed. In the dark of the car, with only occasional headlights from the other lane lighting his face, I couldn't get a read on his mood.

"What's up?"

"Sorry. Sometimes I think too loud. You know, since last year your mom and I have been back and forth about this life you've been thrust into. And now you're in even deeper."

I nodded, even though he probably didn't see it. I'd almost pulled me out of TOS after Denver.

"I accepted a partial promotion. I'll lead the technology development and manage people on the projects, but I won't assign people to teams or to field work. Lorenzo and I talked about it for a few minutes, and it's the best way to go. It'll be announced on Monday." I paused to let him say something, but when he stayed silent, I went on. "I know you and Mom worry. But I love what I do, and it's a pretty amazing life. I'm glad you let me make the choice. It won't be long before it'll be all on me to make these decisions, so I'm glad you let me do that now."

"You know we'll still worry long after you're eighteen, right?"

"I know." I smiled. "Like I worry when you're gone. And, realistically, I'm safer most days than either of you are when you're deployed."

"That's true. There's a certain safety, most of the time, doing what you do in your bedroom."

"Don't make it sound like I'm a shut-in." I chuckled and he joined in. It was a good release from the seriousness of the talk.

"I think you made a good call with the promotion. Handling the tech side is probably enough."

My phone vibrated. It was late for Lorenzo to be calling.

"Speaking of." I held up my phone before I tapped the screen to take the call.

"Winger, Doctor Possible here. Can you talk?"

"Defender's with me."

"That's fine. The bots we deployed to pick up traces of the file have turned up all kinds of pings. They've moved the file a lot. The suspicion is they're moving it from drive to drive in person rather than transferring over the net to be more stealth with it."

"What do we know about the machines the artifacts were found on?"

"Not surprisingly, they're trying to get it decrypted. Several of the IP traces suggest contact with known hackers."

"Do we have anyone we can work with to try and set a trap?"

"Already on that." I should've expected that answer.

"Are the artifacts clustered in one area?"

"The major cluster is in the Northeast from Boston to DC, but someone's taken a copy to the West Coast because we've found artifacts on San Francisco- and Portland-based IPs."

"They've clearly made copies. How are we going to know if we get them all?" I considered scenarios trying to find a way to deal with that, which seemed nearly impossible since it was so difficult to find one whole file. "If you get any leads, let me know. We can talk more tonight if you need me. I'll be in the car with Defender for another hour or so, and then you can always wake me."

"Will do. I'll keep you posted."

"Thanks, Doc."

Once the call disconnected, I typed a couple of emails, cc'ing Lorenzo, since I'd had some ideas I wanted the team to look into since I couldn't.

"You know you take on a whole different tone when you talk to Lorenzo?" Dad stole a glance at me. "It's like you're suddenly a decade older. I think I started noticing that right after Denver." He sounded wistful about this, and I couldn't figure out why.

"Trying to be professional, I guess."

"Or you're growing up." He stole another look at me. "Sorry. Sentimental parent moment."

"Huh?"

"You're not exactly like most teenagers. Even if you take out the TOS stuff, you're sixteen and take college classes. You have a crazy brilliance with technology. You're a major part of the same organization your mom and I work for. Sometimes we have to set aside that you're our son and not even able to vote or drink yet."

If there'd been enough light in the car, Dad would have seen me blushing.

"But there are still moments, regular moments, where you're just my son growing up, and none of that other stuff plays into it." He didn't stop going down this uncomfortable path. "Sometimes it's small stuff like when your voice changed or when you asked me to show you how to shave. Then there's the more obvious stuff, like when I'm gone for a while and come home to find that you're taller or bulked up. Or even taking on more responsibility. Tonight it was that shift in your voice."

I wasn't often speechless, but I had no clue what to say.

As the silence stretched out, I got more uncomfortable. Was *thank you* the right response?

"Don't worry." Dad apparently had superpowers that let him sense that I was overwhelmed. "You don't have to say anything. Just know I'm proud of you."

EIGHTEEN

Saturday morning wasn't nice. Despite the drive, I hadn't relaxed much from the game. It usually takes a few hours to come down from the adrenaline. Usually I went out with Eddie, and when I came home, I chilled with Netflix or something. Dad and I talked a lot on the drive about all kinds of stuff, and I enjoyed the conversation, but it didn't do much to release my energy.

We got to the hotel around eleven thirty. I spent about an hour in Dad's room doing some TOS work since I wanted to check on what Lorenzo reported earlier. When I went to the room I was sharing with Dean and Lars, they were awake and watching hacked hotel porn.

I was impressed by their ingenuity, illegal though it was. I wondered if others on the team had done the same thing—or if they could without Dean. They were polite enough to ask if they should turn it off since I'd arrived. I said no. I didn't need to dampen their fun.

I quickly got ready for bed because my body made it clear that it was time to lie down. I popped in my earbuds to tune out the bad dialogue and moans. Luckily the cot sat low to the floor, and with its position I couldn't see the guys or the TV, which was just a flashing light in the room.

Despite the exhaustion, sleep didn't come quickly. My mind refused to rest and my legs were restless. I didn't conk out until sometime after two.

The wake-up call was unwelcome. Luckily, with two roommates, I could shower last and steal a few more minutes' sleep.

At breakfast the team was ridiculously chipper, and I struggled to put aside my foggy start. Mrs. H distributed information she'd received overnight that outlined how the competition would work.

There were seven teams. Entries were loaded onto a server located in each team's work room. A proctor would be present at all times to make sure there was no tampering. Teams would randomly select a room that would become theirs for the weekend. No internet connections were allowed on the computers, and everyone's phones and other devices would be inside the break room and only able to be used when individuals were outside their workrooms.

Once the competition started, the clock wouldn't stop. After time ran out, teams would return to the hotel where the awards banquet would start at three.

The winners would be determined by points awarded. We'd earn points based on how fast we decrypted entries and by how long it took for the other schools to crack ours.

Alice made a frustrated face. "I don't see anything about bringing notes. Can I bring my print outs?"

Mrs. H read through the information. "It doesn't say you can't, so you can see if they stop you." She folded the papers and put them next to her nearly finished oatmeal. "I want to say how proud I am of all of you. You've made a lot of progress in the past couple of weeks. Now we go for the win. What's our strategy, captains?"

Oh cool. She had them determine how we would proceed today. That was awesome and something I wished I'd thought of.

Dean and Jessie traded looks.

"Six modules and nine of us." Jessie leaned in, speaking quietly so we moved in to hear better. The other teams were in the dining room—it was easy to spot the clusters of teens. No need to give up our strategy. "Each of us should grab a module and try to crack it on our own. That'll give us a first look at everything. If you can't crack what's in front of you, stop and buddy up with someone else. After an hour we'll break and rethink our strategy."

"Theo." Dean looked to me. "We'd like you to take a look at all the modules and let us know which ones you think we can easily knock out and which ones will be more difficult. For the more difficult ones, focus on what you think we need to do to succeed. That okay by you?"

"Sounds good. And I'm around for questions like when we're in class. I have no doubt we're going to take this."

Everyone finished up their last bites, and Mrs. H told us to meet in the lobby in twenty-five minutes for the bus to campus.

I stayed at the table for a few minutes after the others left. It gave me a chance to send off some messages before I went quiet for most of the day.

"Theo, got a sec?" Dean dropped into the seat next to me. I thought he'd gone with the rest of the team.

"What's up?"

"I heard Wes got suspended for a couple weeks and might even get expelled. Some of his thugs got suspended too. All because of you apparently."

I nodded. I'd heard the same. I figured my report was either the final straw or more information had surfaced afterward. "Yeah. Don't worry. I didn't bring you into it."

"Is it true you crushed his junk and took out two others?"

I shrugged. "They came after me and I dealt with it."

This time he nodded. "Thanks for doing what I didn't have the balls to do." I couldn't suppress a laugh. "What?"

"Way too many references to balls for this early in the morning."

"Aren't you supposed to like balls?"

We looked at each other, like we couldn't believe what the other had said.

I tried to look annoyed, but I couldn't. Truth was I wanted to laugh more, but I held it since we were talking about serious things. I went back to what I'd done about Wes. "Look, he needed someone to bring him down a peg or two. He messed with the wrong guy."

"Well, thanks. I'm going to talk to Ms. Cohen on Monday and let her know what he's been doing to me. If you can speak up, so can I."

"Good." I held up my phone. "I need to text Eddie before I'm cut off for the day. I'll see you in a few."

"Yup." He got up and left the restaurant.

I'd figured he would be pissed that I turned Wes in, even if I didn't mention his name. Hopefully Dean would follow through. That would help ensure Wes was expelled, and maybe force him to get help to reform himself.

I texted Eddie.

Good luck at the meet today. Make sure to send me a selfie since I don't get to see you looking all sexy by the pool. It'll be a treat for one of my breaks.

Then Dad.

Enjoy your day! I'll let you know how it's going when I'm on breaks.

Then it was Lorenzo's turn.

No phone most of the day. Text Defender if there's an emergency. He can track me down. I'll check in when I can.

By the time I sent Lorenzo's, Eddie had texted back.

I'll send you something good. I promise. Make sure you kick some cyber ass today (or whatever the right term for this competition is). Catch you later.

I smiled and felt energized despite the lack of sleep.

NINETEEN

THE WELCOME and orientation were brief. It gave us the chance, though, to see the competitors as sixty-some students and teachers packed into a large classroom in the Mudd building on the Amherst campus. Once room assignments were handed out, everyone moved to where the classrooms we would work in were located.

"This is it." Mrs. H stood in the doorway labeled with a two. "You'll do great. You've got a firm strategy, and there's no way any of these schools can beat the teamwork you've got. So go in there and start on the path to a win. I'll see you at lunch."

Inside the room were four tables, each with four laptops. We had more computers than people, which could be a good thing depending on what we were trying to do. Each of the computers had an ethernet cable that ran to a router at the front of the room. The router plugged into a small server that had a monitor connected to it. The screen faced away from us. A college-age guy stood next to the table.

"Good morning. I'm Chet and I'll be your proctor for

the competition. Please leave your phones and backpacks on the table by the door." Most of us had started to do this before he said to. "The only things you can have at the computer stations are the notebooks and pens provided. You can also use the whiteboards that are around the room. Who are Jessie and Dean?" They raised their hands. "Very good. Is this your entire team?"

Our captains looked around at all of us clustered behind them while Alice hastily stashed her notes in her bag.

"Yes," Dean responded.

Chet crossed the room and closed the door behind us. The formality surprised me, especially since we could still come and go from the room. Even the couple of competitions I'd done at MIT hadn't been this strict. I guessed it was because of the amount of money up for grabs.

"If you need to exit for a break, you can at any time." Chet returned to the front of the room. "You can take your backpacks with you, but when you return they must be already closed and returned to the table."

We all nodded and made murmurs of understanding.

"In two minutes, the computers will switch on and you'll be able to start. Next to each are the instructions on how to access entries. Of course, you won't need to work on your own." Chet's enthusiasm was a bit much for as early as it was. His job was to make sure we didn't cheat. Yet he sounded like a spectator at a game, waiting to see his favorite team. "You'll be able to work continuously until two o'clock tomorrow afternoon. That's all you need to know from me. If you have any questions, just ask. Good luck."

"Okay, guys, we do what we talked about at breakfast," Dean instructed. "Theo, will you keep track on the hour?"

"You got it."

"Let's grab a seat so we're ready when the computers come on," Jessie said. "Let's do this!"

Now the team perked up with whoops and hollers. I'd never heard them like this, and it made me feel like I was about to hit the ice. I offered up a hearty "Go Tigers!" and a couple of others followed suit.

Right at eight the laptops snapped on, and we got to work. I decided to pace myself and look at each entry for ten minutes. Even with ones I thought were simple, I planned to go in depth so I'd give good reconnaissance to the team.

The first two left me underwhelmed. It was difficult for me to not break them because of the messy code. I hoped Dean took one of these two in the first hour because he'd knock it out with no problem. These would likely be cracked quickly for most of the teams.

Entries Three and Five were solid. I was glad we'd improved our entry because the original would have paled in comparison to these. Four was in the same class as our entry, but still different. This one would take some time. It looked like each team member from that school put something different on it. It made me think of a door that had multiple locks and chains. If that team was smart, there were decoys too—similar to the idea of not locking all the locks on a door so an intruder might actually lock some while unlocking others.

Six was an anomaly—far more sophisticated than the other five. I wasn't even sure where I'd start with it. If it were a job, I'd unleash several scripts to find its weaknesses, but manually? This might be one that no one gets into. I could build something like this, but would average high schoolers? Could Dean? It's one thing to decrypt, but it's something else to build security on this level. Mrs. H and I certainly hadn't taught these encryption concepts to the team. I'd have to review this one more.

"Yes!" Alice said. Cullen and Lars flanked her at a laptop. "Number two is down, guys."

I grinned, quietly thrilled that it wasn't Dean who'd cracked it. The team gelled so well.

"I'm close on One," said Nat.

Jessie and Dean abandoned their screens and went to stand behind Nat.

"Walk us through it," Jessie said.

Nat detailed what he'd done that worked and what failed. Jessie leaned over and scrolled through what was on the screen. I watched from my seat. If they wanted me, they'd call. The room, however, had stopped working and watched to see if we'd complete another module in the first hour.

"There." Jessie pointed at the screen, and Dean nodded.

Nat looked confused as he studied the screen. "Shit. I don't see what you're talking about."

"Let me sit." Nat moved so Jessie could take over the keyboard.

While Jessie typed, Dean explained. It was perfect teamwork. Several others came in behind to watch. "Got it!" she declared.

"That's an hour guys." I called time and the team applauded.

"Two knocked out in the first hour. Great job," Jessie said, going to one of the whiteboards. She put up columns for one through six and then marked Xs through the first two. "What do we know about the other four? We'll hold Theo's comments for last."

The people who'd looked at Three, Four, and Five all

gave their commentary and were pretty spot-on from my assessment.

"Six is a bitch," Cullen said. "That's why I moved to work with Alice. It's beyond anything I've seen. Even Theo's toughest one for us didn't look like that."

"He's right," I said, deciding to break into the discussion. "It'll be tough to crack Six in the time allotted. I didn't think we'd see anything like that here."

"Can you do it?" Dean asked.

"Eventually, yes, but I'm not sure I can do it by tomorrow afternoon either. I'll need more time to create a game plan. As for the rest of them, your reviews nailed it. In my view Three and Five are very doable. Four is clever and is the closest to what we developed. It'll take time, but I'm sure you guys can get it."

The team absorbed my information and looked ready to go.

"Let's take a quick break," Dean said, and I liked the confidence he displayed. He needed to let himself be like this more often. "Jessie and I will come up with the breakdown of how we want to proceed, and then we can get back to work. Back here in ten?"

The team was in good spirits as we headed out of the room to enjoy time away from the keyboard. Dean, Jessie, and I walked out together, talking quietly.

"Six is a big problem, eh?" Dean asked.

"Definitely."

"How about we put you and me, along with Cullen and Alice on Four and split up the others on Three and Five." Jessie talked fast while we walked. "Theo, can you stay on Six and come up with a strategy on how we can tackle it?"

"Works for me." I smiled, pleased that she didn't want me to hack it for them.

TWENTY

RETURNING from the break room at the end of the hall, we found Mrs. H studying a monitor in the hallway. It hadn't been there when we'd left the room earlier.

"Oh, hey, you guys are doing great it looks like." She gestured at the screen and we looked at it.

The monitor showed how many modules had been broken by each school. We were in a four-way tie for first. Two schools had one and the remaining school had none. At the bottom of the screen was a note: *Leader board only shows how many modules have been hacked. Scoring for timing will be added after the competition is complete.*

"And we're ready to attack three of the others." Jessie sounded full of confidence.

Mrs. H smiled, as if all the plans she'd put in place were executing perfectly. We hadn't won yet, but I guessed she felt pretty good about it.

Back in the room, we got to work. I brought up Six to study it. It was something I might create to secure sensitive TOS information. Is this what it looks like to teachers when a parent helps too much with homework? It's hard to believe they even let it in the competition since it was leaps and bounds ahead of the other entries.

Maybe the team that submitted Six had someone skilled like Dean and me. It almost had to be a single person since it didn't seem possible a whole team of people our age could have this level of skill. I couldn't discount that it might be a fluke too. Maybe it's the infinite monkey theorem in action —left long enough a monkey at a keyboard could code something uncrackable.

I smiled at my weird thought, which evolved into monkeys trying to design encryption.

The code was beautiful, and the more I studied it, the more I marveled at the masterful structure. Nothing resembled a backdoor, but there were some traps waiting for those who weren't cautious.

I'd looked long enough. I decided to dive in to crack it. I didn't want to do the team's job for them, but my review hadn't given me tangible information to tell them.

After a couple hours or so, a recognizable pattern emerged. How had I missed these? Maybe because they shouldn't be here.

I opened my notebook and wrote out what I saw, and there was no doubt.

"Fuck me," I said quietly, but involuntarily.

"Theo?" Dean, seated two terminals away with Cullen, looked at me.

"Sorry, nothing. Missed something obvious. It happens."

"Maybe you should take a break," he said. "You've looked like you want to climb inside the screen. Come talk to us about Four and then check on how the guys are doing on Three and Five. By then we should break for lunch."

"Gimme a few more minutes. Then I'll take a break, clear my head, and work with you guys."

He nodded and returned to work.

I flipped the page of the notebook over and scribbled the same code over again. There was no mistake and yet it had to be wrong.

This appeared to be the missing file.

Not only that, it had Keys's signature in a few places.

It didn't make any sense, and yet it stared back at me from the screen and the notebook.

No way!

This time I managed to keep my mouth shut.

It'd never been brought up that Keys had worked on the encrypted key. I wasn't 100 percent sure this was the stolen file, but it met at least some of the specs I'd received. The bots were designed to look at surface characteristics, things that would be easy to spot quickly if the file was in a directory. Of course we weren't looking too deeply at the code where Keys's signature was.

I needed to confirm what I had. I didn't have the bots with me and, even if there was time, I didn't have the information to recreate them.

Why was this here? Why would anyone think high schoolers could crack it?

A shiver ran through me. What if it was what Lorenzo and I had talked about? Was the weird stuff going on with my phone a way to get to me? Did someone know I'm here? It didn't seem possible. And why would they think I'd just hack it if I recognized it? If not me, someone else? Dean had hacked in the past.

Chet, at the front of the room, couldn't see my screen. But I couldn't risk implementing Wi-Fi on this machine since competitors weren't supposed to be connected to the outside. The laptops were wired into the server at the front of the room, and it was plugged into the ethernet in the wall. The server had to be on the school's network in order to provide information to the standings monitor in the hall.

Depending on the network configuration outside the room, Lorenzo might be able to tap in to review the file and run the bots against it. We weren't going to have much time to figure out—

"Theo?" Jessie interrupted from her seat two rows back. "Can you come have a look at what we're doing? I wanna make sure we're not about to do something wrong."

"Sure." Keeping these guys in the dark was critical. If I'd found the stolen item, whoever put it here would be close by.

I stood behind Jessie and looked at her screen and she explained. She'd mounted a really good attack, well set up to come at the file from two different computers.

"You weren't kidding, this one is complicated," Jessie said. "But it also seems haphazard at the same time."

They explained more of what they'd uncovered that helped form their course of action. I saw what they'd meant about sloppy. It was like the people who worked on it hadn't talked to each other.

I looked through their code for a few moments. "I think your strategy to pull it apart is sound. Each of you take a path, coordinate the final attack."

A woman came in the room and, without a word to us, went to Chet. He'd spent these first few hours reading a book, looking at the monitor next to him, and watching us. As the woman approached, he got up.

"Okay, I'm going to get some lunch. Lauren will be with you for the next half hour or so."

Jessie looked at her watch. "How about we take lunch too and decide our strategy for the afternoon?"

The group agreed. We exited the room and immediately saw signs that pointed the way to lunch.

"I need to check in with a client. I'll join you in a few minutes." I grabbed my backpack off the table so I'd have all my equipment.

"Be quick, okay? We need to know more about Six." Jessie's gaze conveyed her annoyance. I had no choice, though. Lorenzo had to be notified.

TWENTY-ONE

"DOCTOR POSSIBLE, WINGER HERE." I called him from outside the building so I had privacy.

"Winger. I didn't expect to hear from you. I don't have anything new."

"I think I do."

"That's... surprising. Tell me."

"Did Keys work on the encryption for the file we've been hunting?"

"Not that I know of. So much of this mission is need-to-know, though. I'll ask Red Hat and see if she knows or can find out. Why do you ask?"

"One of the modules that's been submitted for the competition has Keys's signature. It's also got characteristics of the file the bots are looking for."

"Can you confirm it's the file?"

"Not with the visual inspection I've made. I'm going to modify my phone so you can use it to home in on the room we're in. The server has sixteen laptops plugged into it, and it's wired into the building's network. You should be able to get in and see if it's what we're after. I have no idea why it's here, but if it is, that means we've got minimum six copies here."

"Solid plan. How am I going to know you're ready for me to start?"

"I'm going on comms."

"I'm impressed. Bringing it with you like that."

"I carry stuff, just in case. Remind me to show you the custom backpack Mom and Dad got me for Christmas. It's got hidden compartments so I can stash stuff."

"Very cool."

"I'll get the phone set up and let you know when I'm on comms. I'll do that now because I need to get back to lunch and work with the team so they don't get pissed off."

"Understood. I'll stand by."

I disconnected the call and went back inside. In the lobby, I sat on a bench so I had a surface to use my laptop. When it came online, I plugged my phone in. I modified the phone so it would appear to be powered off while actually being on and acting as a hidden Wi-Fi hot spot. It was easy to do given my previous work to give me precise control over its functions.

Once done, I inserted my earpiece. Since Denver, I'd become a pro at getting the tiny device in place with tweezers. Using the comms app on the phone, I connected to Lorenzo.

"Doctor Possible, Winger here." I spoke barely above a whisper.

"*I've got you on comms and I'm piggybacking your phone's Wi-Fi.*"

"Perfect." I spoke with my phone to my ear, so it wouldn't look like I was talking to myself. "I'll let you know when I'm back in the room. I'll do what I can to keep the team away from the file."

"Sounds good."

"I'm not going to mute my side. You'll hear a lot, but that might be a good thing. Feel free to silence me if you need to."

"Until we know for sure what's happening, I'll leave the channel open."

"I'm headed back to the team. Look forward to your analysis."

"Thanks, Winger."

It'd only been fifteen minutes when I walked into the break room where lunch had been set up. Luckily I didn't get an evil stare from my teammates when I joined them with a turkey sandwich and Dr Pepper.

A screen with the standings stood adjacent to the tables that held the food. Not much had changed—the school that had zero now had one and another had reached two. Five schools tied in first.

"Everything good, Theo?" Jessie asked.

"Yeah. Things are under control. I told them I'd check in later. What'd I miss here?"

"It sounds like we'll knock Three off shortly after lunch." Dean jumped in with the recap. "I'd like you to join us on Four to offer guidance so we can get that one put to bed. Then we can all move on to Five. We think Six will be the finale."

I nodded and pretended to think that through. "Let me spend no more than another hour on Six. I've got some ideas that might give us a place to start."

Dean looked to Jessie and they nodded. "Okay," Jessie answered for them. "That'll work. Dean and I will split up between Four and Five, then. It'll be a divide-and-conquer strategy since Three is under control with Alice in charge."

The rest of lunch passed and the team peppered me

with questions. Others answered the questions before I could even begin, and I sat there with a small smile of happiness. I'd managed to teach something, and that was pretty damn cool. The questions were also very smart. I wished we got points based on how the hacks were accomplished because I think we would've earned big points. The approaches they used were beyond how they worked when I first joined the team.

I was a proud teacher.

"Winger, I talked to Red Hat." At least I'd used comms enough that I didn't flinch when Lorenzo's voice filled my head. *"Keys worked on this. Apparently we were asked for help to create the security, and she was our liaison to the team. I agree it's probably the file we're looking for. I'll confirm that once you're back at your computer. Of course, we still don't know why it's there."*

"What makes Six so difficult?" Alice asked.

"It's encryption like I'd expect to find for a financial institution." I'd almost said government files, but that got too close to the truth. "It's beyond anything that I put in front of you and blows the other five entries out of the water." I decided to use the analogy I'd come up with earlier. "It's like someone's parent did the work."

"That's not fair," Cullen said. "How are we supposed to beat that? Part of the winning formula is to have an entry that takes a long time to crack."

"Maybe we can complain about the level of the entry?" Alice offered.

"I haven't given up yet. I'm looking for the way I can guide you."

"If we have an entry that's not really fair, why not have you do the work?" Alice pushed.

Even without access to my regular tools, I suspected I

had an advantage knowing some things about how Keys worked, but this was no doubt more difficult than any of her puzzles. However, I didn't want the file opened. I looked to Mrs. H, who watched us but wasn't adding anything. I suspected she wanted to see what the co-captains came up with.

"Let's give Theo some time," Dean said. "When we break for dinner, we can make the plan for how we'll work tonight. We decided we didn't want him doing the work for us."

"But if we've got an entry that's clearly designed by someone who doesn't belong here, why not use our ringer?" Alice demanded.

I kept my mouth shut. In theory I agreed with her, and if I didn't already know what the file contained, I would have gone forward and worked on it.

"Let's keep the plan we've got for now." Thankfully Jessie backed Dean's plan. "We'll regroup as planned."

Alice did not look happy, but nodded.

"Winger, do you know the school that submitted this?"

Looking at the leader board, the names of the participating schools were displayed, but no clues on which file belonged to each.

"Of the seven schools that are here"—I gestured to the leader board—"do we know who submitted the individual modules?" I looked to Mrs. H.

She shook her head. "That'll get revealed at the awards ceremony. They aren't even numbered the same per room. What you're calling Six could be Three for another team."

"This points more and more toward one of these schools submitting something that's not from a student. If a team built Six, they should be ahead of everyone else with the decryption."

"Unless they are deliberately going slower to not show off," Dean added.

"True." I shrugged. I had no doubt Dean held back. If he worked to what I thought his skill level was, he should've hacked another one before lunch—and maybe two.

I pulled my phone from my pack, aimed it at the leader board, and snapped a picture.

"A picture to mark the event and where we were at lunch time." Some of the others decided to snap one too, including Li, who took a selfie with the board. Perfect. Now it wouldn't seem odd that I'd done it.

"Well done, Winger. I'll pull that to see what I can find out about those schools and who's on the teams. Meanwhile, standing by for you to get your phone back in the room."

"All right." Jessie stood up. "Let's get back to it."

TWENTY-TWO

"NO DOUBT, IT'S THE FILE."

It had been less than an hour since we got back from lunch.

"I found it on six of seven servers. I assume the server it's not on is the school that submitted it. I haven't found out what school that is, other than they're in room four."

I bit my lip because it was difficult not to acknowledge him.

"I want to have some limited communication with you. I can see the laptops connected to the servers and the typing that's going on across all of them. Can you type j k so I can lock on to you? It won't take more than a couple seconds. I'm watching for it now."

I followed instructions and he quickly found me.

"Perfect. Got you. Terminal three in room two."

"Hey, Theo, anything?" Dean asked. I'd been so intent on listening to Lorenzo that he managed to sneak up behind me.

"I think I have a plan on how we approach this. I was about to come talk to you and Jessie."

"Cool." He sounded pleasantly surprised. "Mind if I have a quick look? I haven't even opened this one yet."

I slid my chair over, and he dropped into the one next to me and came close to the screen.

He scrolled through the code, and as he did he went pale. When his mouth dropped open, I thought he might throw up.

"Dean?"

His mouth moved, but no words came out. His reaction didn't make sense. No doubt he could see the intricacies of the code and probably even had ideas on how to crack it. But why did he look terrified?

"Dean?"

"We need to talk," he said quietly and stood up before I could reply. "I need a Coke," he announced. "I'll be back in a few minutes."

No one said a word as he went to the door.

"I could use one too. Wait up."

The team watched but still said nothing. It must've seemed odd to them that the two of us suddenly needed a drink when lunch hadn't been that long ago.

He looked freaked. It reminded me of how he looked when he'd hacked my phone and took out the school's computer.

"Dean, what's going on?" I asked once we got to the break room.

His eyes darted around as he took a can of Coke from the container from lunch. The only people in the room looked like teachers. Mrs. H talked with two others, and there were other groups chatting at tables. Nothing looked amiss.

"I've seen Six before," he whispered. "That code. All of it."

What? My mouth dropped open just like his had.

"How's that possible?" I asked when I finally recovered from the surprise. "Do you know someone on one of the other teams?"

He shook his head and lowered his voice further. "Let me be clearer. Locksmith has seen that code."

How did this day get so completely messed up? This was supposed to be a relatively easy weekend, and it turned into ground zero for a high priority mission. And what did I say to this non-TOS person?

"What did he say? Is he one of your teammates? Damn, you can't give me a clue. You moved away from your keyboard. I'll keep listening."

My mind raced. I had to keep my cover, which meant I knew nothing about the origin of the file or its importance outside of this competition.

"I don't understand. Why would you have seen someone's entry before the competition?"

"Last week. Someone I used to hack with. She sent me a message to get my help." Dean sounded freaked and his compulsion to look around the room only intensified that feeling. "I hadn't talked to her in months because she got too aggressive. For her, hacking became about stealing and making statements rather than some fun and pointing out security holes. But... shit. Mrs. H is coming over."

He turned, grabbed a cookie off the table in front of us, and took a bite.

"Everything okay?"

"Just needed a pick-me-up," I said as Dean tried to look normal, but failed.

"You sure? Dean, you don't look well."

"I'm fine, really. I, uh, didn't eat enough at lunch."

"Okay. Don't spend too much time out here. A couple

schools have moved ahead, so you need to keep up the pace."

"I'm going to the restroom," I said, "and then I'll get back to it."

I hoped Dean would follow so we could talk more, but it gave me a few seconds with Lorenzo.

"Locksmith is a hacker. You'll find stuff on him in the files." I spoke very quietly knowing the comms could pick up even the slightest whisper. "Dean tried to hack my phone during class, and in my analysis of what he did, I discovered his alter ego. I'll keep digging on why he knows about the file."

"Understood. Standing by."

Once in the restroom, I looked around and found no one else. It didn't take long for Dean to show up. Once again, his eyes darted around.

"No one's here."

Unless it's bugged, it suddenly occurred to me. And I had nothing on me to detect for that.

"Anyway," he said, jumping into the story, "Violet Knight wanted me to help crack the file that's here as number six. I took one look at it and knew it had to be something important. I had no interest in hacking it. She offered to pay 20K, and that was the other clue that she shouldn't have it."

"You didn't tell anyone did you?"

He looked ashamed, then looked away. "No. Besides, if I came forward as Locksmith, I can't imagine that would end well. I never stole, but I broke into systems."

From my research I knew Locksmith had no active investigations, but I couldn't tell him that. It was one thing for me to know he was Locksmith. He didn't need to know that I'd read files on him.

"I've got a team on Violet Knight to see if we can track her down for questioning. Might be able to get info on who put the file out there."

"What are we gonna do, Theo? What if someone's coming after me? They had to know I'd recognize it."

"Maybe we leave it. We don't have to crack all of them." I thought quickly, and this was the best option so the secret list didn't get out. "No one knows if you really can or not. Violet could've overhyped you, right?"

I stayed deliberately nonchalant in an effort to calm him down.

"I'm scared, Theo. Violet told me they were pissed that I wouldn't try. I don't know if they forced her to tell them more about me. I...."

"Wait. She *knows* you? In real life?"

He looked away again. He clearly wanted to be anywhere but here. Hackers, like covert agents, usually worked with screen names to stay hidden. Too much knowledge could be dangerous.

"Yeah. We.... Never mind. It doesn't matter."

"If you're in danger, it does. We need to tell Mrs. H."

It wasn't a great plan, but if Dean was in real danger, he needed to get somewhere safe.

"No." He scowled like he hated the idea as much as I did. "Maybe if I hack it, this will all go away."

"You'd said no before. How can this be the right choice now?"

"Violet Knight is Romy Nelson from Providence, Rhode Island. An agent is headed to her last known address." Lorenzo hearing everything made this much more efficient than it might otherwise be.

"Look, let's get back and work on the other modules." I offered up an alternate plan because his sucked. "Let's focus on what we're here to do. I'll keep looking at Six. Maybe there's a trap in it, and I can *accidentally* vaporize it. If not, we'll talk after dinner. We're two smart guys. We can figure this out, right?"

Dean nodded slowly and bit his lip, looking unconvinced. I clapped him on the shoulder and headed for the door.

"Let's go." I held the door open and he walked out. He wasn't the confident team captain he'd been earlier. He needed to find a way to turn that back on because we didn't need the entire team wondering what happened.

"Check that out." He pointed to the monitor in the hallway outside the classrooms. "We racked up another one." That improved his mood.

"Sweet." We were one of three schools that had a third module completed. "Let's get at least one more done before dinner."

"Yeah. We can do that." Sometimes his ping-pong moods confused me, but I was glad he found a way to be upbeat again.

"Where were you guys?" Jessie asked, barely looking up from her screen.

"Sorry. We got caught up talking strategy on Six and lost track of time."

"At least you were busy."

Dean sat down where he'd been working. "Great job cracking another one too."

"Some of us weren't slacking." Alice winked at him before she headed for the door. "I'll be back in a few."

"Can you get to your computer so I can ask some questions? Use j k again when you're there."

"I'm going back to Six. I'm determined to find a way for us to handle it."

Dean nodded as I sat down and pressed the keys.

"Is it possible Dean knows more than he says?"

I typed: *Maybe, but I doubt it. Seems freaked.*

"We're watching the module on the other servers too. We need to come up with a plan once you can safely get away from the group. I've briefed Red Hat and Defender and deployed more agents to your location since whoever's behind this may be there."

While Lorenzo had spoken, I'd deleted my original message so there'd be no trace. I'd have to do this each time I typed to him.

My response was simple: *Understood.*

"I'll be listening in case anything else comes up."

I typed: *OK*

"I thought we'd divide and conquer on the two that are left aside from Six," Jessie said once Alice returned. "If we can knock those out tonight, we can all attack Six in the morning. What do you think, Dean?"

"Let's do it." Dean looked at me as if I might have something else in mind. Which was weird because we wanted to stay away from Six anyway. "Theo, you'll coach us on these while we work to make sure we're on the right track."

"All right," I said enthusiastically. Buying in to the team's plan would be a great way to let time pass while Lorenzo gathered more info.

We got to work, and over the next four hours, the team knocked out Five. We made progress on Four too but decided to leave it for after dinner.

TWENTY-THREE

"Defender and Shotgun are in room 204 if you can get there. They're also on comms."

That was unexpected. I knew Dad had gotten a briefing but, even though he was in the area, I hadn't expected him to be on-site or for John to make the trip from Boston.

We'd been at dinner for about thirty minutes and talked about our Four strategy for most of the time. I figured Four would take most of the night. It'd proven to be more complex than my initial review revealed.

Once the chat moved away from the competition, I decided to take time away from the team.

"Guys, I need to check in with my client again. I'll either see you here or back in the room."

"See you in a few," Jessie said.

No one looked upset this time.

On the second floor, I found 204 quickly. I tried the doorknob and found it locked.

"Defender, Winger here. I'm outside 204."

The door opened enough for me to slip in.

"You've had a busy day," Dad said. He had a slight

smile, which he often used when there were tense situations that were going well.

"Hey, Theo," John said with a nod.

"Sorry to blow up your quiet weekends. Any updates?"

The room was a computer lab, similar to the one the team was in. There were no laptops on the rows of tables, but there were places they could be plugged in for power and internet. Dad and John had their laptops at a table nearest the door, but were using one of their phones as a hot spot for security.

The laptop chimed with a video call.

"Winger, Defender, Shotgun, Doctor Possible here. Let's go over everything quickly for Winger." His voice came through comms rather than the computer, which eliminated echo.

"Yes." Dad took over. "We've got five agents in the building with three watching the competition space. When Dean's out of the competition room, we'll always have eyes on him. We're continuing to gather information on the competitors, their parents, and teachers to see if there could be any connections to the file."

"I'll be able to watch Dean in the room, and it'll be easy for me to move with him if he leaves."

"You said you don't think he's more involved with this than he says, right?"

"Right. He was too freaked when he saw the file—like he'd seen a ghost."

"We can't eliminate the idea that he knows more," added John. "After all, you're deceiving him too, and doing quite well it seems."

John was right. I couldn't let my thinking be clouded because I sort of knew this guy. Truthfully I didn't know that much.

"Stand by, please. I'm getting some information." We watched Lorenzo talk to someone offscreen.

"You doing okay, Theo?" Dad asked.

"Yeah. I'm fine. I'm confused about how the file has ended up here. Other than that, I'm good."

He nodded and gave me his "I'm a proud dad" smile.

"Sorry about that." Lorenzo looked at the camera again. *"Violet Knight has been found severely beaten in her apartment. The local CSI have her computers, but we've got someone en route to secure them for us. We've also got ears on her interview with local police. I'll keep you all updated."*

"It's reasonable to believe that the person who wants this file decrypted is here," Dad said. "They wouldn't allow it to be opened and then leave it on a server as part of a competition."

"Unless someone at the school that submitted it plans to transfer the file directly from here." I agreed with Dad, but we had to consider a transfer might happen from here even if it would put the data into the open. "Of course, the way the competition computers are connected, a transfer wouldn't be the easiest thing either. Doc, do you see anyone else in the system like you are?"

"No. And we're monitoring for that."

"What's the plan, Doc?" Dad's question surprised me because he was the senior agent present.

"With so many students and other civilians nearby, I'm tempted to suggest the plan Theo threw out with Dean earlier—do nothing, let no one hack the file, and let the competition end. The other schools are continuing to stay away from it. Meanwhile, we work to find who's behind it and apprehend them while they're close."

I didn't like it. There was no guarantee we could find who put the file here before the competition ended. We had the chance to put a stop to this now, and it felt like we should be more aggressive. Dad still didn't speak up, so I did.

"While there are a lot of students, we also have to be aggressive and recover this file while it's here. We still need to find out which school put it into competition. The sooner we do that the better. I'll start talking to other competitors too and see if I can get any clues."

I paused a moment for any discussion. When there wasn't, I continued. "If we can't sort it out tonight, I say Lorenzo and I hack the file in the morning and see who comes after it. Even if there are other copies in play, if we hack one, it's a safe bet the person that put it here will want to collect it. Let's get more agents here so we can manage whatever happens."

Dad looked to John and they nodded. "It's risky given our public venue, but I agree. This is the best chance we've got right now." I was proud Dad agreed with me so completely. It was silly to feel that way, but I couldn't help it.

I recognized Lorenzo's conflicted expression. *"Okay. But, above all, the safety of civilians must come first."*

"Absolutely," Dad said.

"I need to brief Red Hat. I'll be in touch when I know more. Winger, I'm on comms for the duration."

"Thanks, Doc." The video chat ended.

I looked to Dad, still confused why he wasn't the lead.

"What?" he asked.

"Why aren't you the mission leader?"

"While I have seniority overall, this is an IT mission. Lorenzo's in charge unless he turns it over to someone else. As one of his senior agents, you certainly have more to say on this than we do. Make no mistake, if I had something to contribute or felt that a mistake was being made, I'd speak up. But you guys are doing fine." He clapped me on the back.

"Yeah, you're doing great, Theo." John put out his fist and I bumped it.

My phone buzzed with a text message. I looked and it was Dean searching for me.

"I should go talk to Dean."

"Okay. We'll be here," Dad said.

"Cool. Talk to you soon." I headed out.

I fired off a text to Dean: *On my way to the break room.*

"Received word from our agent following Violet Knight." Lorenzo's voice filled my ear. *"She had a relationship with Dean so she knows a lot about him. She was assaulted two days ago and told the guys that did it all about Dean and where to find him. With her injuries and her equipment smashed, she couldn't get help. They basically left her for dead, and somehow she hung on until the postman tried to deliver a package and she cried out loud enough for him to hear."*

"Wow. Okay. We're gonna have to keep him safe. Once I'm back with him, I won't let him out of my sight."

"Ranger has been posted in the hallway the competition rooms are on. He's in a campus security guard's uniform so it won't be a problem for him to be there. He knows what Dean and you look like."

"Have him join comms too. Just in case."

"He's already on."

Dean paced near the break room and looked up as I came downstairs. "Can't talk anymore." I barely moved my lips in case Dean paid close attention.

"Understood."

"Jesus, Theo, where were you?"

"I told you, I had work to do."

"Yeah, I know that, but *where* were you? I looked everywhere."

"I was upstairs so I could talk without interruption. That doesn't matter. What's freaking you out?"

He gripped my left wrist and took me to the end of a hall that was away from the competition. Even with that he talked softly. "I tried to get in touch with Violet Knight. Her computers are offline, which makes no sense. I called her cell and ended up talking to a cop."

"What'd you say?"

"Are you kidding? I hung up. How do I know she's a real cop? What if it's something to do with that file?"

I decided to play dumb. "We should really tell Mrs. H. She'll know what to do."

"Against these guys?" His voice grew more hysterical even while he whispered. "What's happened to Violet that a cop answers her phone? Why's her equipment offline? She never turns that stuff off."

"We're in a public place, surrounded by a lot of other people. There's no way they're going to come after you here."

Hopefully he wouldn't overthink his safety.

"Seriously? You were snatched off your bike in broad daylight last year."

Dammit.

"Even more reason why we need to tell someone what's happening," I said, changing my tactic.

"Who's gonna believe me?"

"I believe you."

"Only because I was stupid enough to tip my hand to you," he said, getting more agitated.

I pointed to the guard I assumed was Ranger. "Look, there's security right here."

"Winger, Ranger here." A new, very deep British voice sounded off in my ear. *"That's me you pointed at. I'm about to adjust my hat so you'll have double confirmation."*

The guard didn't take his hat off, but he moved the brim up and down.

"Has he been here all day?"

"I don't know about him, but I think there's been one around, yeah." I had no idea if there'd been another one, but I needed Dean to chill.

"Let's get back to work, okay? We've got one more we know we can crack before we have to think about the other one."

"Do you have a plan?" Dean spoke quietly when we walked by the guard.

"I've thought about how we can appear to work on it while making sure we don't actually open it. Given what you've said, I agree that it should stay locked."

TWENTY-FOUR

SHORTLY AFTER ELEVEN we decided to take a break. We'd been told there'd be a major snack spread from ten to one, so it was a good time to check it out.

Once we opened the classroom door, we heard thumping music from the end of the hall where the break room was. I saw Ranger pacing the hall. Since the rooms were along the first floor's central hallway, it made his job easier to keep watch.

"What's going on?" Cullen asked.

"No idea." Alice started to groove to the music as we walked.

We stopped in the doorway of the break room and found it full of people. When we'd been here for meals, there'd been some other students, but it looked like all the competitors were here, given this looked like the same size crowd from orientation this morning. Some of the teachers were here too. We'd stumbled on a hacker party.

People were grouped together, most likely by team. Time to take advantage of the chance to meet people and try to sort out which team submitted Six and maybe find out where they got it. I followed our team to an open table.

"What's the music?" Lorenzo asked.

"Someone turned on music in the break room." Ranger provided details. *"It seems most of the students decided it was break time."*

After a few minutes of talking team strategy, I made my move. "I'm gonna get some food."

"I'll come with," Dean said.

"Me too," Alice added.

Not what I wanted. I really needed to be solo for my investigation.

The food looked decent—hamburger sliders, wings, bite-sized pizzas. Perfect late night nosh. I loaded up a plate and looked for a good place to plant myself so I could hear as much as possible and watch the room.

I hung back so the others would go back to the table. I stood near the tub where the sodas and water were iced. Three clusters of students were nearby, and I could hear bits of their conversation.

"Winger." It was Lorenzo. *"The module belongs to West Springfield High School. They're in room four. Nothing odd has come up in the background checks for anyone associated with the school. We're still looking."*

My teammates spotted me, and Jessie and Dean headed my direction. Dammit.

"If you've got pictures of that team, send them to my phone so I know who I'm looking for?" I said quietly, my mouth obscured by a slider.

"Will do. Stand by."

"You're not coming to hang out?" Jessie asked. "There's more to talk about."

"Sorry." I tried to sound extra apologetic. "I need to

stand for a while and try to stretch out my legs a bit. They get restless if I'm too still the day after a game. Being awake this long doesn't help either."

There was truth to what I said—I could hurt after a game. So far, I felt okay despite the amount of sitting I'd done, but standing couldn't hurt.

Jessie nodded. "I've got aspirin in my purse if you need some."

"I might take you up on that. I'll do some stretches once we get back to the room. That'll help too. Give me a few minutes and I'll come sit." I smiled and bit into another slider.

Dean stayed behind after Jessie left. "Were you able to—"

"Hey. You're Theodore, aren't you?" Someone came up to us. He was shorter and smaller than Dean and me and wore a Batman comic T-shirt along with blue jeans. I couldn't imagine why he broke away from his team to talk to us. "You go to MIT, right? You were part of the early admission panel last fall."

Wow. I hadn't considered I'd see people from that here.

"Theo's got fans," Dean said. At least he could focus on something besides the file for a moment.

"Yeah I was," I said to the stranger.

"Way cool. I'm Gavin, by the way." He grabbed my hand and shook it quickly. "I got accepted to take some classes this summer. I'm surprised to see you here. I would've thought this was way easy for you."

I shrugged. "There's some tricky stuff here. That one that looks like a dozen people did different things is challenging."

"Yeah, man. We've had three people on that most of the day."

"What have you worked on?" If he was accepted into summer classes, he might have some insights.

"They've had me stuck with a crazy one. Wait, did you design that one that's crazy hard? This competition's like the three bears. Two modules that are too soft, one module that's hard as a rock, and three that are just right."

I chuckled. His analogy was on the mark. "I've been on the rock most of the day too. It's ridiculous."

"You can't crack it either?"

"I've taken a cautious approach. I don't want to trip anything with the wrong move."

He nodded. "Yeah. I've been careful too. I'm trying to find out who made it to say congratulations because I suspect no one will hack it. So far no luck, though. But, it's cool to meet you. What are you working on these days?"

"I'm doing research on information warfare using computer viruses and cryptology."

"Scary stuff."

"Very. In the fall I'll be part of a team Dr. Shorofsky's put together to do a year-long research project. That's why I'm already looking at the topic. I don't want him to regret picking me."

"I saw his discussion too. He's incredible. I think I only understood half of what he said. I can't wait to start. Will you be taking classes in the summer?"

"*Pictures are in your phone, Winger. Digging deeper, we've found that Douglas Benjamin's father works with a Russian-based research firm that has often been suspected of espionage. We've got no proof he's involved, but it's a lead. Benjamin's picture is the first on your phone. We're pulling pictures of the father and checking hotels to see if he's in the area.*"

"I haven't decided on classes yet. I'll prep for fall, but I may take the summer off."

"Maybe we could hang out sometime? I'd love to hear more about your work."

"Sure. You can look me up in the student directory."

"Sweet. Okay, I'm gonna see if I can find the school that dropped this piece of code on us."

"It's not that table." I pointed to where McKinley's team sat. "That's my team."

"Great. More people eliminated. Catch you guys later." He was full of enthusiasm and stepped immediately over to another group of students.

"Do you have a lot of groupies?" Dean asked.

"Not that I know of." I scanned the room.

Dean's phone rang and it startled him. He remained unhinged, even though he was trying to be calm. His expression clouded over when he read the screen.

"I need to take this." He walked away, heading out of the room.

I pulled out my phone and brought up a listening program and tried to look into Dean's phone.

"Damn it," I said softly.

I'd run into his phone's security, and I didn't have the time, or the best tools, to deal with that. He wasn't gone long, and he looked shaken when he returned.

"That was Violet Knight." He spoke softly, so much so that I had to lean in. "She's in the hospital because some guys beat her up. She told...." He shuddered. "She told them about me to make them stop. She wanted to warn me."

"Shit. Do they know you've seen the code?"

"Maybe I should get out of here."

"No." I gripped his arm. I couldn't let him run off. He'd be too vulnerable.

"Let me go, Theo," he said, sounding on the edge of panic as his voice wavered. I suspected he'd make a scene if I didn't act fast.

"Look, you're safer here," I spoke softly, trying to calm him. "They've gone this far to get you to do this thing here. There's no reason to think they'll do something extreme if you can't crack the code. But if you walk out, they could grab you and.... You don't want to end up like Violet."

His gaze bore into me. I had no idea which way I really wanted him to go. If he walked, TOS would keep an eye on him. But if he left, we'd lose the best chance we've had yet to end this.

We stared at each other. I worked to project some level of tranquility by loosening my grip a bit and not looking flustered. His eyes were a mix of fear and determination.

Finally Dean dropped his shoulders and looked to the floor. I released my grip. "This doesn't seem like the best idea."

"You're doing okay, Winger." Dad picked the right moment to give encouragement. *"He is safer here where we've got more people around than he can see."*

I caught sight of Gavin. While he talked to another group of students, he subtly pointed to the person next to him. It looked like he mouthed the words "it's him."

Gavin did it. At least he thought he did. I hadn't had a chance to look at the pictures to see what Douglas looked like.

"Looks like Gavin may have found the guy who submitted Six. Let's go see if we can find out anything useful."

"Why would we want to do that?"

"The more information we've got, the better chance we'll make the right decisions."

168

He sighed but didn't move to follow me.

"You can come with me, stay here, or hang with the team. It's up to you." I finished the food on my plate and tossed the garbage in the can. I left Dean alone. After a couple of steps, I turned to see what he'd decided.

Dean shook his head and went to sit with the team. That made things easier.

"Winger here." The more I did the quiet talking, the easier it got. "Is someone in the break room that can tell me if I'm joining a group with Douglas Benjamin? I haven't seen the pictures yet."

"Hey, Theo." Gavin sounded excited. "I found the team. They're responsible for that crazy thing we're working on."

"It's really all Dougie." As a goth guy spoke, a boy I could only describe as a beanpole, decked out in jeans, white T-shirt, and well-worn denim jacket, shrugged. He looked young, younger than a freshman.

"Swordmaster here. I'm in the room as one of the food servers. You probably guessed by the name, but he matches the photo of Douglas Benjamin."

"You got skills, man," I said.

"Yeah, we're lucky to have him," Goth Guy said.

"You did it on your own?" Time to get on with the prying and see what I could get away with.

"Yeah. We each built a module and then voted on which to submit." He didn't sound like someone who'd built a winning entry. I'd expect at least a little cocky attitude.

"You gotta admit," Goth Guy piped up, "Dougie's is beyond anything else here."

"It rocks, man." Gavin went into fanboy mode. "I'd love to hear how you designed it. I've never seen such well layered encryption."

"I'm not talking to the opposition." Dougie crossed his arms over his chest and gave Gavin and me a look that dared us to ask another question.

"What about after?" Gavin asked.

"Yeah, I'd love to understand the techniques you used." I piled on in hopes of getting some answers.

"Yeah, maybe. You probably wouldn't get it, though."

Two adults approached from behind Dougie.

"Swordmaster here. The taller of the two approaching is Laurence DeMayo, the school's computer-science teacher. The woman is unidentified."

Interesting. Mr. DeMayo I'd seen earlier with the other teachers. I didn't recall the woman, and I think I would've remembered her stern, imposing demeanor if I'd seen it before.

"Sorry to interrupt," Mr. DeMayo said. "You all should get back to work. There's only fourteen hours left and we've only cracked half the modules so far."

Sounds of disappointment came from the team, especially Goth Guy. Douglas, however, looked ready to go. They said goodbyes and departed. The stranger scanned the room as she left, and Dougie stayed closer to her than his teammates. There was something weird about those two. I hoped someone would follow to see if they did anything before returning to their room. I couldn't ask since Gavin stood by me, and I didn't know where Swordmaster was to even shoot her a glance.

"I hope he talks tomorrow," Gavin said. "I doubt my team will open that file, so I really want to know how he built it."

"Well, I'm going to get back to it." I gave a nod to Gavin. "Later! It was cool to meet you."

I made my way over to the team. "I'll see you in the room."

"I'll go with you," Dean said, standing.

"I'm addicted to the wings," Jessie said between bites. "I'll catch up." Several others at the table indicated the same.

So much for seeing Dad and John. At least if Dean was with me, he wouldn't be running off.

"Was that him?"

"Yeah. His team is enamored, so I guess he's got skill. On the other hand, I know they're actually behind us since their teacher said they still had three modules to go. If they think he created that module, I wonder if they're confused about why he hasn't been able to hack the others?"

"Maybe he's like me?"

I made a face at him. "If you're hiding, you don't pass off something like Six as your own."

"True." We got back to the room and found Chet chatting with another guy. We stayed in the back of the room, dropping off our stuff on the back table. "What do we do now?"

"Go back to work on Four. We'll deal with Six later."

"You know we're going to end up with everyone looking at it. Jessie thinks she's close to figuring out Four."

"I'm not surprised. And it's fine when it happens. If we start to work on Six, I don't imagine they'll get far, and you and I will even give misdirection if we have to."

Dean nodded. He still looked nervous, but at least he was calm. I was confident with TOS around, they'd figure out what to do to bring this to an end before we had to do any work with Six.

TWENTY-FIVE

JUST AFTER TWO in the morning, I told the team I needed to stretch my legs. Up in 204, I saw Dad and John. Somehow neither looked very tired. They were working on identifying the woman that Douglas Benjamin stayed so close to. There were no leads yet, which was peculiar because it was easy to dig up something on most people.

Lorenzo and I hatched a plan. At eight, we'd work together on Six to see if anyone would surface. They had to be monitoring, and if we could draw them out, that might work to our advantage.

As I went downstairs, Eddie buzzed my phone.

It was a sweet message: *Here's an "I love you" before going to sleep.*

And I happen to be on break! Up for a phone call?

Neither of us liked to text if we could talk instead. I imagined him on his back, in bed, glasses still on so he could read.

Of course.

Quickly I brought up the comms app on the phone so I could stop transmitting.

"Winger here. Muting transmission for a few minutes."
I tapped to complete the action.

"Understood," came Dad's reply.

I dialed Eddie and walked outside. He answered on the
first ring.

"Hey," he said in his sleepy voice.

"Hey. You sound exhausted."

"Yeah. Shouldn't have gone to the movies, but with you
out of town, some of the single guys on the team insisted I
join them."

"That's cool you went. Get some team bonding in."

"I'd rather be with you."

"Same here. Things are pretty good. We're tied for the
lead and we've got a handle on all the entries except for one
that's a bitch that I'm not sure anyone will crack."

"Are you going to handle it for them?"

"I'll help, yeah."

"So are you locked up in a room most of the time?"

"Mostly." The crisp night air felt good. I sat on one of
the benches and folded my legs under me. The position felt
great as it stretched my quads. "Met some people from some
of the other teams earlier during a break. They're cool."

"I know it's Sunday, school night and all, but you wanna
hang when you get back? Maybe I can throw my parents
out for a while?"

I couldn't help the dopey smile on my face. Eddie was
sweet, and he'd developed a wicked sexy streak too. Our
first time naked was so tentative. We understood the basics
but didn't quite know how we fit together and what we
liked. These days we knew exactly what to do with each
other.

"I'd love that. Perfect end to the weekend." He let out a

contented sigh. "Oh, don't do that. You're gonna make me sleepy and want to curl up next to you."

"Plenty of room for you to slide right in."

"Now you're just being mean." I imagined myself doing exactly what he suggested.

"Mean is if I did this." Sounds of him adjusting the phone filled my ear, but I couldn't tell what he was doing. When my phone pinged with a text I had a suspicion.

"Hang on," I said before he could say anything else. I opened the text. "Oooh, look at you." He must've propped the phone on his nightstand somehow. The picture showed him lying on his side with the covers open as if he were inviting me to join him. The sleepy eyes behind his glasses and one eyebrow raised were so cute. His smile warmed my heart. Then there was his swimmer's body—only covered by light blue boxers—that took my breath away.

"Glad you like it."

"I do. I think that needs to be my wallpaper, or maybe a calendar," I said, referencing the Christmas present he'd gotten from Mitch a few weeks ago.

He hummed an appreciative noise. "Don't you go showing that to anyone else."

"Why not? They'll be jealous at how hot my boyfriend is."

He chuckled. "Show me you."

"I'm not nearly as interesting." I held the phone out and flipped to the camera so I could take a selfie. I had nothing to prop the camera on so I held my arm out, made a kiss face, and snapped.

"Awww. I think you look more tired than I do. You gonna make it?"

"Yeah. There's plenty of Dr Pepper here."

"I know you're set, then." Eddie yawned, and I had no choice but to do the same. "Sorry."

"It's okay. I should let you go so you can sleep."

"Yeah, I don't wanna be the guy who falls asleep on his man. Good luck finishing. Let me know as soon as you win."

"You say that like it's a for sure thing."

"*Please*. I'm sure it is." I laughed softly at the sass in his voice. "Love you, Theo."

"Love you too, Eddie. Good night."

"Night."

He disconnected and I navigated back to his picture. Probably the cutest selfie he'd ever taken. Everything, from the smile to that raised eyebrow, said come snuggle with me.

Back on the comms app, I reactivated my transmission and told the team listening that I was back. I stayed on the bench, deep in thought on Six, for about a half hour before I rejoined the team.

TWENTY-SIX

SHORTLY AFTER FIVE THIRTY, the team unlocked Four, which took longer than expected, making it even more satisfying. Five modules were completed and only Six loomed in front of us. As we exited our room, we were greeted by the best news possible—we were the first school to unlock five entries. A couple of schools had four, but we were alone in first place. There were still hours to go so it looked good for us, but there was the unknown of how our entry was standing up to hacking by the other teams.

In the break room, we all got egg sandwiches and coffee. The team deferred to me to lay out how we'd work on Six.

We got back to our room about seven in good spirits, even Dean, as the competition's final seven hours began. I gathered everyone around the whiteboard along one side of the room, and I wrote out the high-level concepts around which Six was built.

We did this like we had in the classroom. We projected code on the whiteboard at the front of the room. I drew diagrams and talked strategy while the team listened and asked questions. Even Chet paid attention, changing seats so he could see the code and what I wrote.

"Look at what's happening here." I pointed at the screen. "If you—"

A scream ripped through the air. Muffled shouts followed. It was close. Perhaps near the break room.

"What was that?" Alice asked as we all looked toward the door.

"Winger, Ranger here. Three entered the lobby fast. The woman leading them is the one who escorted Douglas Benjamin out of the break room. A teacher was shoved forcibly into a wall. I'm intercepting."

Chet headed toward the door.

"Winger, I'm also pursuing. They—" Swordmaster began. *"We've got weapons drawn. One of the men is—"*

I flinched as a gunshot rang in my ear as well and echoed in the hallway. Swordmaster went quiet.

"Stop!" Ranger shouted. *"Campus police."*

Two more shots in the hallway. Closer.

What was happening?

"Doctor Possible here. Remember we've got students and other civilians. We need to protect them at all costs even if it means we lose the package."

Screams and yelling were right outside the room. Chet reached the door, but hesitated.

"Chet, lock that. Now!"

My shout spurred him into action, but the door burst open. He caught it in the face and chest and staggered back, falling to the floor. The team dropped for cover when a woman and two men with guns raised entered.

"Winger?" Several people called my name at once.

"It's okay," I said quietly as much to the team around me

as to those on comm. "We stay calm and find out what's going on."

"We're here for your teammate." It was the woman who'd been with Douglas. Her accent sounded British, or maybe Irish. I wasn't sure. "Get on your feet. All of you!"

We stood slowly and the team huddled together.

"Him." She looked as stern as ever pointing with her gun. The other two, who were obviously in the role of henchmen, came for Dean.

My teammates grabbed on to each other. Dean's hand locked on to my shoulder with far more intensity than I thought possible.

"No. No. No." Dean got louder as they came for him. He pulled on my shoulder, and it hurt as he dug in until they forced him to let go.

More commotion outside the room. A male voice strained to sound calm as he shouted into the room, asking what they wanted.

"Police have arrived and are setting up a perimeter," Dad said.

"We've got what we came for." Stern Woman spoke to someone in the hall that I couldn't see. "Do not interfere." She slammed the door with so much force that it shook the wall adjacent to it. She locked the door. It appeared to be a flimsy lock that could likely be breached easily.

"Up against the wall, all of you," Stern Woman said gruffly.

No one moved from their position.

"Come on guys." I pulled Alice back since she still held on to me. The group moved so we ended up against the whiteboard we'd used.

"Listen to him. He's a smart one."

"Oh my God, Chet!" Alice shrieked. He was out cold, sprawled on the floor. He bled from a cut on his forehead.

"He needs help." I stepped forward, but Jessie pulled me back. "We can't just leave him like that."

"Yes we can," Stern Woman said in a chilling voice. It was clear that she wasn't going to be deterred from her mission. "Now, Dean Brody, it's time for you to work on this file. We hoped you'd get it done yesterday, but with time running out, we decided to focus your attention."

"I can't do it." His voice shook.

"Is that why none of us know what to do with that?" I asked calmly. Despite being stuck in *typical teenager* mode, I refused to play into the fear these guys were creating. "I told you that didn't come from a student."

"*He* can," Stern Woman said, waving her gun in Dean's direction. "And he will."

"What's she talking about?" Jessie asked.

"You don't know about your teammate? He hasn't solved all these problems for you? He has a reputation for getting into places he shouldn't. He should be able to release the information we need from this file in no time."

Chet moaned and struggled to sit up. "What happened?"

Goon One quickly went to Chet and knocked him in the head with his gun. More blood spilled near his ear, and he fell back to the floor. The team gasped and there was at least one yelp.

"*Winger, give us clues if you can,*" Lorenzo instructed. "*We should have eyes on you within five through the laptop cameras.*"

"This man needs help." I got out of Alice's grip and moved away from the team.

"Get back," Stern Woman said while Goon Two cut me off from getting to Chet.

Three bullies in the school bathroom were easy to handle. I couldn't risk anything like that here with guns involved and others who could be hurt.

"I'm going to help him." I focused on using my work voice, the one Dad commented on last night. "No one needs to die while you're doing whatever this is with Dean."

Stern Woman nodded and Goon Two stepped aside. Kneeling next to Chet, I checked out the gash on his forehead, which was clotting. The side of his head was far worse off with blood coming from his ear and a wound on his cheek.

I took a deep breath through my mouth. I had a hard time with blood. The smell of it made me sick. I didn't need to get woozy while this situation unfolded.

"You really did a number on him." I looked at Goon One standing over me, and he gave me an icy look. "I need something to stop the bleeding." I looked around to see if there was a first aid kit in the room. There wasn't.

Since I wore a T-shirt over a long sleeve, I pulled off the tee.

Goon One tensed up as I brought the T-shirt over my head like he thought I might have a weapon.

"Winger, we've got eyes on the room. We deactivated the web cam lights so no one can see they're on. We've patched this to Defender and Shotgun, who are at the on-site command center with the police."

Sounded like TOS and the police were already teamed up. There were TOS agents embedded in law enforcement all over the world. Plus TOS agents often served in many federal agencies. Dad had Department of Homeland Security credentials.

"Now, Dean, have a seat and let's get to work." Stern Woman acted like this was the most normal thing to do as she pushed Dean into the nearest chair. "The sooner you get this file open, the sooner your friends can get on with their day."

I worked on Chet, lifting his head gently to wrap my T-shirt tightly around his head to stop the bleeding. I opened each of his eyes, and his pupils were responsive to the light. That was a good sign. I looked around the room again and found what I needed.

"Cullen, I need your hoodie."

"Sure, man." He stepped away from the wall and took it off.

"Did I say you could move?" Goon Two aimed his gun at Cullen, and he stepped back. "He needs the hoodie, he can come get it."

"You've got Dean, why keep the rest of us?" I asked, mostly to see what the response would be.

"Winger, be careful," Dad said in my ear. *"I know what you're trying to do, but you don't want to antagonize them."*

"Don't you watch movies?" Stern Woman said. "It's always better to have hostages. Even better if they're kids."

I quietly got the hoodie from Cullen and returned to Chet. I made the hoodie into the best pillow I could and put it under his head.

"Now, Dean, what do you need to be able to get this done?"

"Let me look it over. I'll need some time to see what I can do with it."

I returned to the team and didn't know what to do. Should I volunteer to help? Should I let Dean do it solo? Would he unlock it since we agreed it should stay locked? Getting out wasn't an option. We were well covered with

Stern Woman near Dean, Goon Two guarding the team, and Goon One at the door.

"Don't give me that shit. You had a good look when Violet asked you to take the job with her."

"Winger, we can see you," Lorenzo said. *"Can Dean hack this file? If you think so, make a fist with your left hand."*

I fisted my left hand. It would likely take him a while, but I knew he could do it.

Dean visibly shook. "But I don't know how—"

Stern Woman yanked Dean from the chair by his shirt while Goon Two moved to restrain him. Stern Woman aimed her gun at Dean's chest. Some of the team gasped. Cullen and Alic looked away. Goon One quickly moved nearer the team.

"Dean, don't," Alice squeaked.

"Don't bullshit me. Violet made it very clear you could do this and that you decided not to."

"Leave him alone." I stepped forward. "He says he doesn't know."

Goon One punched me in the stomach, and I dropped to my knees. Stupid that I hadn't anticipated a response like that. I wrapped my arms around my midsection and stayed down, while keeping my eyes on Dean.

"I... I need him. I need Theo's help." Dean looked at me, an apology written across his face. Was he worried I'd say no? "He's even better than I am."

"Then get over here, Theo." Stern Woman gestured to a seat next to where Dean stood.

I stood slowly, wanting to seem more hurt than I was. I glared at Dean. I wanted everyone to think I was pissed, but the setup worked perfectly because I'd be more able to control the situation in front of a keyboard.

"We're right here with you," Lorenzo said. *"We're monitoring all of the laptops so we see everything."*

The only mystery was I didn't know how fast or slow Dean could get into the file. If he went too fast or did something wrong, he might prevent me from being able to do something meaningful to end this well.

Goon One shoved me toward Dean.

"I want this file opened within the hour or one of your classmates will pay the price."

Dean and I looked at each other. I shrugged and nodded. We had no choice but to get to work.

TWENTY-SEVEN

"WINGER, *Defender here. We've got some information on the woman holding your team. We've debriefed with Douglas Benjamin. His father was abducted earlier this week. Douglas and his mother were told if he turned in this module to the competition and allowed this woman to chaperon him, his father would be released. She called herself Julie Carson, but based on what we can find, that's an alias. We're working on her exact identity.*"

This just got weirder. Dean and I weren't special. If we couldn't decrypt this file, there were a lot of people who could. Why come after Dean? If they wanted a student, why not a college student? If they were willing to pay Violet Knight and Dean, why not pay someone else? Or was it because using a student made them think they'd get away with it?

I stole a glance at our teammates, clustered close to each other against the whiteboard. All of them looked scared, a few wept.

One of the phones on the table at the back of the room

rang. Initially Stern Woman ignored it, but it kept going. Whoever it was seemed to be leaning on the redial button.

"Winger, Shotgun here. The cops are trying to get them to pick up the phone. The one they're calling is the only one that's on."

I wasn't sure what they hoped to get from that, but it'd be something.

Stern Woman took the bait. "Whose phone is this?" She held it up.

"Mine," Cullen said weakly.

She went up to Cullen and showed him the display. "Do you recognize this number?"

"No."

Stern Woman pressed the screen to take the call. "What?" She listened for a moment. Whoever was on the phone wasn't on comms.

"I've got what I need right here. This will be over within the hour because I need to be on my way. And if they can't do it, well...."

Dean stole a look at me and I shrugged.

I typed a quick bit of code so I could type onto Dean's screen from my computer.

We need to just get this done, I wrote.

And then what?

I don't know. Hopefully it ends.

"Oh, I'm afraid Douglas's mother is a widow since he violated our agreement." She paused again. "I have all I need. Once these boys decrypt this file, I'll go."

So they were willing to kill. We needed to hurry this up.

"Shotgun here. Douglas didn't indicate he thought his father was dead. Not sure if it's a scare tactic or reality."

"What's taking so long?" Stern Woman raged and threw

Cullen's phone against the wall. "Maybe you need a clock on this to spark your competitiveness. Or perhaps some other incentive?"

She gestured toward the group and Goon Two grabbed Alice and Jessie.

"Let me go," Jessie said, struggling against the man's hold. Alice shrieked as she was jerked forward.

"Hey, you—" Goon Two let go of Jessie long enough to punch Cullen in the face. He fell backward into the wall, holding his nose. Lars and Nat stabilized him.

"Here's the deal, you've got thirty minutes before I hurt one of these two. I'm going to leave it up to my friends what they do, but I assure you the ladies won't like it. Now get to work!" She bellowed loud enough that I figured people in the lobby heard it.

Dean and I cringed. Stern Woman had no patience and that made her dangerous.

"Doc, how fast can we get that file decrypted?" Defender asked.

"Winger and I should be able to do it in the time frame. We've been writing bots here to assist. If we involve Dean, our speed might increase. We can't separate what he's doing from us without him knowing it. But Winger can direct him."

Lorenzo gave me an earful of instructions. I simply took it in and started and occasionally told Dean things to do. He followed directions flawlessly. He showed off some mad skills along the way too.

What really sped this up were the scripts Lorenzo had produced. Dean and I could've done this on our own, but the half hour requirement would've been difficult to meet.

"Winger, one of the students is on the move toward the

door," Defender said. *"It's a very bad idea. He's in a red and black shirt and has black hair. That's all we can see."*

Cullen was either trying to be a hero—or save himself.

"You there, stop!" shouted Goon Two.

"Cullen! I need you over here, please." I shot him a glance over my shoulder. If I could make him useful, maybe—

"What's wrong with you?" Stern Woman blazed with fury and moved past Goon One to get to Cullen. "Your friends are gonna get hurt, just like that one," she said, gesturing at Chet, "and you're trying to sneak out?"

"Sorry. I didn't... I can't—*Ahhh!*"

I turned. Stern Woman broke Cullen's right wrist. I knew how to do that, and if it was done right, it guaranteed Cullen a long recovery period. Stern Woman shoved him toward the group.

Cullen whimpered as Lars caught him and lowered him to the floor.

"I won't be so gentle to the next person who tries something stupid," Stern Woman growled.

"Guys." The quiver in my voice annoyed me. I hadn't realized how nervous I'd become. "Let Dean and me finish." I looked at Jessie and Alice in front of me and then back to the rest of the team. "Then this will be over."

"Keep listening to him. Now, smart guy, open the file!" She stood in front of me and screamed directly into my face.

"You're doing good, Winger," Dad said. I'm glad he thought so because I had a hard time seeing a solid course of action.

It only took another five minutes of work to open the file. Dean looked surprised. What did he think was going to happen? Of course we were going to open the file. It wasn't acceptable for anyone else to get hurt.

"It's done," I said, looking at Stern Woman.

"Let's see what we've got." She came around behind Dean and me. The file directory had a single entry —*current.dbs*.

TWENTY-EIGHT

"*WINGER, Defender here. MI-6 informed us that the woman in the room is an agent of theirs gone rogue three weeks ago. Her name is Fiona Coyle. This mission's now expanded to recover the file and her.*"

Stern Woman had a real name. She was even more dangerous than I'd given her credit for. MI-6 were very well trained.

"Let's see if you've done your job right." Coyle reached over us and typed a sequence to open the file. A single line of text appeared on the screen: *Open failure—Unauthorized copy.*

Coyle slammed her open hand into the side of my head and nearly knocked me out of the chair. I let out an *oomph* of surprise. She ripped Dean out of his seat and held him by the shoulder—like she wanted to use a Vulcan nerve pinch.

"What did you do?" Coyle asked, menacingly. "Fix it. Now!"

She shoved Dean back into the chair with so much force that he fell out the other side. His ribs crashed into an adjacent chair before he dropped to the floor.

I righted myself, despite my fuzzy vision.

"What do I have to do to make you take this seriously?" Coyle moved her gun between Jessie and Alice. I hated the fear in their eyes. "Do I shoot one of your friends?"

"No!" I said firmly.

Dean tried to pick himself up.

"I told you if you didn't have this done, it would happen." Coyle moved and kicked Dean down and planted her foot on his chest to keep him on the floor.

I stiffened. Maybe if I rushed her and aimed for her center of gravity—

"Winger, you can't win this battle, so don't even try to take her," John ordered.

"It's not our fault." Facts were all I had to stop her. "With security in place to guard against copies, nothing we did would prevent this outcome. The file's contents would've been rewritten immediately when the copy occurred."

"Pick one of them, I don't care who." Goon Two pulled Jessie forward. She tried her best to be defiant and calm, but her eyes gave away how scared she was. Coyle continued, "If I shoot her in the head, she'll splatter all over your friends. Will that make you get this done?"

I hoped counselors were on standby. My teammates weren't likely to forget this anytime soon.

My vision cleared, and I could see what my teammates probably wouldn't notice, and from the angle on the cams, TOS probably couldn't see it either. Coyle had the gun's safety on. She bluffed big-time—at least for now.

In a ballsy move, I grabbed her shoulder and spun her around as much as I could, given the odd stance she had with one foot on Dean. "You wanna shoot someone, shoot one of us since you don't like our work." I gestured to myself and Dean—who looked at me like I'd lost my mind. "There was no other outcome possible since you gave us a copy. You want the information, give us the original."

She put the gun in my face, inches away from my nose.

"Winger!" Dad screamed in my ear, and I hoped no one in the room heard it. *"What the hell are you doing?"*

I held her gaze, thankful I didn't sound as scared as I felt. "Otherwise, we've done what you asked, so you need to let us go."

Coyle's fury was palpable—chest puffing and nostrils flaring. She made no move for the safety, and her men stayed in place.

She poked the gun barrel into my chest. "You're right, this is a copy. We'll give you access to the original, but we're not letting your friends go until you open it."

We stared each other down—a game I was getting pretty good at. I decided to press my luck. "At least let the injured people go and let all of us use the restroom. Otherwise, we do nothing."

"Good job, Winger," Dad said. *"Even though you're scaring the crap out of me."*

The stare-off continued until she finally took a step back, off of Dean, and lowered the gun. "Get me that phone I used before." Goon One scrambled to fetch it from the floor. "What's the code for this," she yelled to Cullen, who was in shock and nonresponsive.

"I can unlock the phone, but I'll need mine to do it." If I could hang on to mine once I was done it might be useful later.

Coyle eyed me.

My nervous voice from earlier was gone. I was far more worried for the team than myself.

"Get it."

I helped Dean up before I made my way to my backpack on the table. Goon One kept close watch.

"Winger, if you can pocket your phone that will give us additional tracking on you." Defender and I were on the same wavelength. And he was back to sounding more like an agent than a dad.

I looked at the team while going to the back table. Jessie looked slightly less scared. Everyone watched me like I'd grown an extra head. Could I justify my actions as some sort of survival instinct?

I returned to Coyle and accessed the app I needed. I reached to take the phone from her, but she didn't let it go.

"I'll hold it. You just do your thing."

The app screen displayed the map of the phones that were in range. As I unlocked Cullen's, the screen flashed, and at the same time, I disabled its locking mode in case we needed it again.

"Done." I tried to pocket my phone, but she grabbed my hand.

"That's a fancy app. Where'd you get it?" She looked at the screen, which only showed the success message.

"I made it."

"Hack people's phones often, eh?"

I shrugged, channeling Dean.

She grabbed my phone and held it, placing it on top of Cullen's.

"Watch them," she told Goon Two who still covered Jessie and Alice.

Coyle put her gun into a shoulder holster inside her jacket and put her finger on the button at the bottom of the phone to exit the app.

"Don't do that!" I reached out for the phone, but it was too late.

The screen went red, and a black circle with a slash through it appeared. With the unauthorized touch while the phone was in secure mode, it immediately bricked itself.

"Why would you do that?" I whined for effect. It sucked the phone was dead, but not the end of the world either.

"Unlock it." She threw the phone at me. "I want to see what a boy genius keeps on his phone."

"It's wiped," I said, keeping up the annoyed tone. "I can only restore it from my home system."

That was a lie. It had to go back to the TOS labs to be rebuilt. For security, no one could resurrect a phone from a remote location.

"Fucking teenagers." Coyle threw my phone against the wall and it dropped to the ground near the team. "Get these two secured to travel."

"Wait. What?" Dean finally snapped out of his daze.

"You're coming with us—both of you." She flipped through Cullen's unlocked phone and tapped the screen to dial.

"*Sorry about the phone, Winger,*" Lorenzo said. "*Sounds like you're going to be taken to the file, which is good. We'll track you with your chip.*"

"Hey, what are you doing?" Goon Two yanked my hands behind my back. Before I could do anything, I was zip-tied.

"*Winger,*" Dad said, "*the plan is to let things play out. Crack the file so she knows it's real and lets you go. We don't want to crash the place while there are civilians present if we can avoid it. Your first job is to access the list so she can see it, and then to protect Dean and any other civilians in play.*"

I had my orders, and I was expendable in an effort to

complete the mission and save others. I couldn't imagine what it took for Dad to give me those orders.

I watched Dean get his hands zip-tied and shot him a look to say this would be okay. I wasn't sure I succeeded, even though I believed it. This scenario was a million times better than what I dealt with in Denver.

"We're leaving," Coyle barked into the phone. "We're bringing four of these kids with us and that's not negotiable." She paused. "We've only injured a couple so far, but we'll do more if we have to." Another pause. "That's it. We'll move when my driver is at the door."

"Winger, take the laptop you used," Lorenzo said. *"I've put the scripts on it in case you're cut off from the internet. You can say you wrote them to speed up the work and it'll be faster to have them than to rewrite them. Plus I've got tracker code in the laptop. If you're on the internet, we'll find it immediately."*

Good thinking. That'll give TOS the cam to watch through too.

Coyle dropped Cullen's phone on the table and pulled one from her pocket. "We're ready. Come to the front door of the building." Coyle looked at Dean and me. "All right boys, we're going out the front door and to a black van. You're going to give us no trouble. To ensure that, we're going to take these two lovely young women with us."

Great. More civilians.

Alice and Jessie got zip-tied. Alice squirmed, but Jessie talked softly and calmed her down.

Coyle's phone buzzed, and she looked at the screen. "Let's move." Dean and I were pushed toward the door.

"I need my laptop," I said.

"We've got plenty of computers."

"I need the scripts I wrote. It'll be faster to have them."

"Fine, bring the fucking laptop." Coyle pushed us toward the door. Goon Two disconnected the cable from the laptop, closed it, and tucked it under his arm.

The halls and lobby were clear.

"Orion here in sector two. I've got eyes on Winger and the group." I didn't recognize that voice, and I didn't see anyone but took comfort that someone saw us.

The black van gave me pause. It'd only been a few months since I'd been snatched off my bike and stuffed into one. At least this time I was, sort of, going by choice.

We got in and, surprisingly, they left Jessie and Alice on the curb. One less thing to worry about. We sped off and they blindfolded me. I assumed Dean got one too. They didn't want us to know where we ended up.

TWENTY-NINE

WHEN THE BLINDFOLD came off we were inside a house.

Coyle was right about the computers. There were a lot. The living room and dining room had scores of laptops and desktops on folding tables. No one was working at the terminals. In fact, no one else was present. It didn't take much imagination to see these machines manned by programmers, or hackers, to do Coyle's bidding.

Our zip ties were cut, and Dean no longer looked scared but rather defeated. I had no way to tell him why this was going to be okay.

Coyle's phone rang. "Get them set up," she said to her men as she left the room. "Yes, ma'am?" was all I heard before she went out of earshot.

Goon Two put my laptop on one of the tables while Goon One nudged us toward the chairs.

"Get these ready to go," Goon Two said. I opened the laptop and booted it up. Dean sat at one that was open and running.

Coyle came back in a few moments with another laptop. She put it on the table in front of us. "The file is the only thing on here. Get to work. Our time is up. The person who bought the list is on the way, and we don't want her waiting."

Why weren't Dad or Lorenzo commenting? It was major that we could apprehend the person who bought the information.

"We need to connect to that." I pointed at the laptop with the file. "Should we use Wi-Fi or do we wire in?"

"Ivan?" Coyle shouted. A guy who looked to be in his early twenties hurried into the room. He wore black jeans and a T-shirt for a band I'd never ever heard of. "Get these laptops connected."

"Yes, ma'am."

Ivan quickly made the wired connections through a router. It wasn't clear if we were on the net or not. I'd know that soon enough if Lorenzo told me he could see the laptop.

"Done."

I got to work. The sooner we opened the file, the sooner this would end.

"Same as before?" Dean asked before I'd made too many keystrokes.

It was a relief, like a bit of weight lifted off, when he spoke even with the quiver in his voice. At least he wasn't off in shock somewhere. Hopefully he'd be able to keep his head in the game. While Lorenzo and I had done much of the work to hack the file before, Dean still had an instrumental role. I hated that he had to go through this.

I examined the file and it looked the same as the one we'd hacked earlier.

"You remember what you did?"

He nodded. "I think so, yeah."

"You better remember, kid. You do not want Melinda

angry." Coyle moved away from us, muttering, "Life was so much easier when all you had to do was steal papers and kill a courier."

Still nothing from Lorenzo, Dad, or anyone else. Something failed. Dad and Lorenzo had talked to me during transport. They tracked the route with my chip and stayed far enough behind that Coyle wouldn't know she had a tail. There was no apparent reason that comms would fail. But I'd heard nothing since we were brought in the house. Possibly they were being quiet so we could get the work done, but I'd still expect updates on the takedown plan. Something might be blocking the transmission, although the comms were supposed to be resilient to blocks. I had no way to check the connections. The laptop I worked on was offline too, so, until I knew otherwise, I had to assume we were on our own.

Given the plans I knew about, however, I had to proceed and hope the chip worked to get them to this house.

I turned to Dean. "Let's do this."

We got to work. I activated the scripts and began the tasks I needed to do. With the clock ticking, I didn't hook into Dean's laptop to keep tabs on him. I simply checked in verbally from time to time.

Just before the half hour mark, I had the file name displayed like we had before.

current.dbs

"It's done," I said. Dean gave me a nod.

Coyle got so close she bumped my chair and I felt her press in against the back of my head.

She reached around me and typed in the commands to open the file. Organization names, usernames, passwords, and other security information scrolled up the screen. The file contained a huge amount of data.

"No," Dean said quietly while he typed a few keys on his keyboard. "This isn't right."

Sparks flew from the laptop we were connected to and the data on my screen disappeared.

"What did you do?" Coyle bellowed.

"Whatever that is, you're not supposed to have it." Dean was defiant and it made me proud, but this was so far off any script that I needed to think fast to catch up.

The computer with the list continued to spark and hiss, and the power in the house flickered.

Coyle raised her gun to Dean's head. "Fix it."

"It's unstoppable until that computer is fried," Dean said, calmer than I'd heard him in hours.

The smell of melting plastic filled the room and smoke rose from the laptop. I'd never heard a computer screech like that. Goon One unplugged it from the outlet, but given the laptop had a full charge, it didn't turn off. Goon Two threw his jacket over it in an effort to control the smoke.

Coyle's thumb released the safety. "Don't test me, boy." Her voice quaked with anger.

Flames crept around the edges of the jacket, and then a loud pop sounded, though it was muffled under the covering. There were several ways Dean could fry the laptop, and I appreciated he wanted to do something to stop this. The men worked quickly to put out the fire that had engulfed the coat.

With Coyle's back to me and the goons distracted by the fire, I slowly closed the laptop I'd used and detached the ethernet cable. In a burst of movement, I stood and slammed the laptop into Coyle's head. It mimicked the move I almost used on Coach during the practice drill. This time there was no safety word. I hit her with everything I had. She stumbled, holding her head with her free hand.

Dean stepped back so Coyle wouldn't run into him. I dropped the laptop. Coyle staggered but I grabbed and spun her around. She needed to be disarmed. I took her wrist and twisted the same way she had Cullen's. Feeling the bones crunch in my grip was horrible. She shrieked and released the gun. She wavered and I let her go so she'd drop to the floor. I kicked the gun and it skittered under a table out of reach.

Her goons didn't seem to know what to do—put out the fire or help Coyle. Maybe no one had ever challenged her quite like this before, so they were dumbfounded.

The front door crashed in and people swarmed the foyer. The backdoor may have been breached too, judging by the noise elsewhere in the house. Dean yelped and went pale as if his courage from moments ago drained away.

"Get down!" I screamed at Dean while men entered with weapons drawn.

Gunshots rang out. I recoiled from a bullet hitting me in the left shoulder. I cried out from the pain and dropped to a crouch to shield myself behind my chair. I saw someone in a suit, standing in the entryway, collapse to the floor, holding his arm.

"Winger?" Dad was back in my ear after the shooting stopped.

"Winger, here." I kept my voice soft, even though I doubted I'd be heard over the shouting. There were more gunshots upstairs and someone, who looked like he could've been another one of the goons, tumbled down the stairs. A police officer intercepted him.

Dean hid under a table. He sat, knees pulled up and hands over his head. It reminded me of the way we were told to sit for tornado drills in elementary school.

Goon One and Goon Two were disarmed and on the ground, restrained.

Two officers were over Coyle, who lay unconscious, one wrist curved at an odd angle.

"Eyes on Winger. He's injured, but conscious." I recognized the low voice as Orion.

Cops along with women and men in suits swarmed the room. It was impossible to tell who was who.

I adjusted to sit cross-legged. Warm blood trickled down my left arm and the smell gagged me. I breathed through my mouth as much as possible. I didn't look at the wound because that would only make me feel worse. I had to know what Dean had done so Lorenzo could hear it.

"Shit, Theo. You okay?" Dean was suddenly at my side. When did he even look up, much less move?

"Been better." I pressed my right hand against my shoulder to try to stop the bleeding despite the pain. "What'd you do?"

"I knew you didn't need me to hack the file. You mostly did it on your own before. So I worked up a way to destroy it. I s'pose it worked out good these guys decided to show up."

"Well done." Wooziness hit me hard. Shock.

"Heard that, Winger." I loved hearing Lorenzo's voice again. *"We'll secure all the laptops. We've got agents in there, which you probably already figured out."*

"We need to get you guys out of here," a cop said, approaching with his partner. He was on comms so I heard the voice with a slight delay in my ear. "We've got a stretcher coming in."

He kneeled and moved my hand so he could press gauze against the wound. His extra pressure sent shock-waves of agony down my arm and across my back. "I'm

Officer Morrison. I'll be with you at the hospital until your parents can get there."

"Winger, Morrison is Drummer Boy. You're good with him." Dad was on hand with the important information. Why did he sound distant, though?

I looked at Morrison and nodded.

"Let's bag up these computers," said an officer in a CSI vest.

"Do you have jurisdiction here?" Morrison asked, looking up.

"CSI Conolly." She flashed a badge.

"Winger, Drummer Boy, Conolly is also with us along with her entire team. She's Dragonfly. She's not on this comm channel to keep it clearer."

"Very good," Morrison said. I leaned into him and couldn't right myself. "Whoa there. Let's lay you down."

Before I knew it, I was lying on my back. I craned my head so I could see Dean. I needed to keep an eye on him.

"Which computers were you boys on?" Conolly asked.

"He used, um, that one." Dean pointed to the one I'd dropped after I'd hit Coyle. He stuttered over some of the words. "I was here. That one," he said, pointing at the charred machine, "had the file on it."

I wanted to reach out. Maybe squeeze his arm to offer support. I felt too weak to lift my good arm, though.

"Someone did a number on this." She walked over and looked at the melted plastic.

When was the fire put out? I hadn't paid as much attention as I should've.

"Yes, ma'am, I did," Dean said with a slight smile despite the fact it looked like he was shaking.

"Let's get you out of here," the officer with Dean said.

He flinched when the woman reached for him. "Your parents are waiting back at the university."

Two medics brought a stretcher in. They lowered it and lifted me on to it.

"Wait." Dean stopped along with his escort. He came over as the stretcher was raised to take me out. "Thank you. You saved my life. She would've shot me for sure. It was insane you beaned her with the laptop."

"You were pretty insane too." Dizziness rolled through me. I sounded weird. Slurred.

"We should get him to the hospital," someone said. Who was that?

They rolled me out. Morrison was at my side. He got into the ambulance and sat next to me. I saw Dean get into a police car.

"Who's Dean with?" I asked.

"The officer he's with is also TOS. He'll—" Lorenzo's voice was distant and then gone.

THIRTY

I HATED WAKING UP FUZZY. The disorientation spooked me.

The light was low, and monitors beeped nearby. My eyes attempted to focus and I tried to move; pain radiated from my shoulder and I could sense it was immobilized. A moment later, Mom and Dad came into view, although it was like seeing them through gauze.

"Theo, so good to see you awake." Mom gently moved the hair near my forehead.

"Hey."

She nodded and smiled. "I don't like it when the first call I get when I'm on the ground is that my son's been shot."

"Sorry." I tried for a smile, but I wasn't sure my face worked correctly. The drugs were strong.

"It's okay." She smiled brightly. Only in my family could getting shot earn you a smile. "I hear you've been busy."

"Little bit, yeah."

There was a lot I wanted to ask, but I couldn't focus on one thing to get words out. They kept looking at me.

Mom playing with my hair was nice.

"What's up with my shoulder?" I finally formed some words.

Mom and Dad looked at each other. The news wasn't good.

"You've been in surgery to remove the bullet." Dad gave me the news. "There's some muscle and tissue damage that'll take time to heal. You'll start physical therapy in a couple weeks."

I nodded. Dammit. The hockey season. A shudder rocked me hard. Even if the Tigers went all the way, I probably wouldn't make it back for the playoffs. Warm tears rolled down my face. I tried to wipe them away, but couldn't figure out how to get my good hand out from under the sheet.

"Shhh," Mom said, moving the sheet out of the way. I wiped with my hand, but I didn't seem to make any progress. "Shhh. Theo. Wait." Mom gently took my arm and laid it by my side. Dad handed some tissues to her and she wiped my face. It was like I was two and not able to take care of myself. Which I guess I wasn't.

"I can tell that you've done the math on that." Dad put his hand on my leg and squeezed.

"It sucks," I warbled. What was wrong with my voice?

Again silence. Mom messed with my hair. I closed my eyes and took some deep breaths trying to steady myself.

"Dean! Where's Dean?"

I jerked and pain shot through my shoulder. My mind cleared. I was in the hospital. Surgery. No hockey.

"Easy," Mom said, coming into my field of view. She stood at the side of the bed, lowering the rail. "You fell asleep. We're right here." She sat down and Dad was doing the same on the other side. I calmed my breath while both of my parents looked at me with so much worry and love etched on their faces that I didn't know what to do with myself.

"Is Dean okay?" I finally asked.

"He's debriefing with a lot of agencies. We've taken responsibility for him and have an agent with him every step of the way. It's been made clear he's not to be treated like a criminal despite his past. He risked himself to keep that list secure, and that goes a long way to wiping out his other deeds."

I nodded. He was okay. I'd done my job to protect him. Mom's phone chirped and she went to get it across the room.

"Did you get the woman who bought the file?"

"No," Dad said. "We think she saw the raid in progress and fled. Based on what we've pieced together, Coyle worked for Melinda DeMain, an information broker. Intel says she had bidders in North Korea, various Middle Eastern countries, and Russia vying for the information."

A soft knock at the door drew our attention.

"Come in," Mom said, which was good since I wasn't sure my voice would carry that far.

Eddie poked his head around the door. "Mr. and Mrs. Reese, hi."

"Come on in, Eddie." Mom went to him, drawing him in the room. She gave him a quick hug.

Oh, wow. He drove all the way here? Was it still Sunday? It had to be. They would've told me otherwise.

"We'll leave you two for a few minutes," Dad said, getting up and going to where Mom was.

The three of them talked for a moment. I couldn't hear. Seeing Eddie was good. It made me warm and fuzzy that he'd haul all the way out here to see me in a hospital bed. He must love me a lot.

Mom gave Eddie another hug before she and Dad left the room.

He came to the side of the bed where Mom had sat, on my good side. "Jesus, Theo, I leave you alone for one weekend...." I chuckled and winced. "Are you okay?"

"I guess. I'm still pretty drugged."

He leaned over and gave me a quick kiss on the forehead. That was nice. I kinda wanted more, but I didn't really have the energy either.

"What happened? I've only heard what's on the news."

Crap. I didn't know the official story, or if anything differed from the actual news. I decided to tell him the truth as it might've seemed to Dean. It was also the easiest for me to tell while I was still under the influence of the drugs.

"Dean's a hacker like you?"

"I am not a hacker. I'm a digital security consultant."

He looked at me with that super cute cocked eyebrow. It seemed to be higher over the top of his glasses than usual.

"What? I am."

He sat on the edge of the bed and held my good hand gently in his.

"You are so loopy right now." He smiled at me and that warm feeling ran through me again. Eddie was much better for me than the actual drugs. "How long are you laid up for?" He shifted topics.

"I actually don't know. Physical therapy's in two weeks, and I'm probably out the rest of the season."

"Why do I think you're already looking for a way to rush the therapy."

"Maybe," I said through a sheepish look.

"Don't get yourself hurt worse." He was strict, pulling out a tone I hadn't heard before. "You gotta stop going to competitions where there are other schools participating. You got hurt in Amherst. You got hurt in Denver. Maybe you don't travel well?"

I chuckled. "Maybe. I'll certainly think twice before I do it again." We sat quietly, holding each other's gaze. A small, adorable smile played across Eddie's lips. "I'm sorry you came all the way out here just to sit on my bed."

"That's what boyfriends do, right?"

"I'm glad it's what my boyfriend does."

"You're taking this pretty well." He squeezed my hand tighter.

"I'm under the influence of some really excellent drugs." I gestured with my head toward the IV, and then I winced because it tugged on my shoulder. "Anyway, it's impossible for me to be too upset right now."

"It gives you a super adorable look on your face too." He pulled out his phone. "Let's capture this. And let everyone know you're okay."

He maneuvered himself into a good selfie position and snapped. He turned the phone so I could see.

"Oh God. That's what adorable looks like to you?" I looked stoned out of my mind, not to mention how unflattering the hospital gown looked with its tiny blue and yellow polka dots.

He sat up. "Totally." He typed and talked while he wrote a post. "You can't keep a good man down. Theo's doing okay. Who knew a computer-science competition could get so intense? #BrokenWing."

"Nice touch there on the end. I might use that hashtag for the next few weeks. You know Mitch is going to be the first to comment on that."

Another knock at the door and it opened a bit to reveal the nurse. "Excuse me. I need to do some checks. She came over to the IV machine and pushed buttons.

"I suppose I should go since it's a couple hours back. Plus you need to rest so you can come home." He stood and we looked at each other again.

"I love that you came out here and I love you." I tugged on his hand and he caught on that I wanted a kiss. "Text me when you get home?"

"You got it." He leaned in for another kiss. This time a soft one on my lips, and it made me forget everything for a moment.

"Love you." He grinned at me before he slipped out the door.

"Love you too." It never got old saying that to him.

"I didn't mean to rush him away," she said.

"It's okay. He's got to get back to Boston anyway."

Crap. I don't have a phone. That memory came rushing back of how it'd been sacrificed.

While the nurse checked me out, I drifted. Eddie's visit was awesome. I couldn't believe he drove for two hours to see me for a few minutes. Although, I'd do the same for him. The one advantage of not being able to play for several weeks would be hanging out with him more. It'd be weird watching games in the stands with him, though.

Mom and Dad were sitting across the room, talking quietly. I couldn't make out their words while my eyes fully focused on them.

"Hey." I coughed and cleared my throat. "Hey," I managed to say louder.

They came over, this time standing next to each other at my bedside.

"This came for you." Dad reached behind Mom and produced a phone from the table. "Lorenzo says it's configured to your last cloud backup."

Lorenzo was a wizard sometimes, getting me phones whenever I needed them. Now I'd be able to get Eddie's text later.

"Lorenzo wants to talk to you once you feel up to it."

I nodded. "Maybe a little later."

"That's fine. He knows you've only been out of surgery a few hours."

"How's Cullen and the rest of the team?"

Dad and Mom traded another look, and this one said that the news wasn't good. Dad sighed. "Cullen's got a shattered wrist and broken nose. He's been in surgery. Chet Kilgore, the proctor, passed away from the head injury. The rest of your teammates are significantly shaken, but physically they're okay. The other students and teachers are also okay, including the one Coyle assaulted when she first entered the building. The civilians were quickly evacuated from the building when she took over your room."

I didn't know what to say. I'd done what I could for Chet. I turned away from Dad and Mom to stare out the window. Cullen had tried for a hero moment and paid for it.

"You have to know that none of it's on you. You did good work."

"I know. In some ways it worked out great because we

got the file secured. For my teammates, though, this isn't the weekend they expected. At least I've been through weird before and know how to process it."

"TOS is providing a counselor for your teammates, families, and anyone at the school who needs one. Dean has one specifically assigned to him as well. It'll keep whatever stories come up close to us—even though we're pretty sure there are no TOS security issues. You did a tremendous job playing both sides."

"I'm so proud of you." Mom ruffled my hair more and I sighed. It was just about the most soothing thing ever. She was taking all of this so well. After Denver, maybe it'd gotten easier for her too. "You didn't break your cover, but you did what was needed."

I nodded. "I tried."

I was rapidly losing the fight to stay awake. I needed to call Lorenzo, but my body didn't care.

"Let yourself sleep, Theo." Dad must've seen my struggle. "Everything can wait and we'll be right here."

I smiled, at least I think I did, before drifting away.

THIRTY-ONE

I DIDN'T GO BACK to school until Thursday. The hospital released me on Tuesday afternoon, and then Mom and Dad wanted me to spend at least a day getting used to my left arm being immobilized by a crazy sling contraption.

No way around it, this was a bitch. I'd been injured before—both in hockey and in the field. But none of those injuries were this severe. There'd be no biking, no hockey, and no lots of other stuff for at least a month.

Thankfully physical therapy started in eleven days—I was counting down to the second when the appointment was. I could ride a stationary bike and walk a treadmill starting next week. Being so still made me crazy, though, and I was already restless.

Eddie was on his way to swim practice, and I was leaving school after wrapping up a meeting with my physics teacher about the test I'd missed. As I approached Mrs. H's classroom, she stepped into the hallway and looked like she was about to pull the door closed. She looked haunted.

"Theo," she said softly, "it's good to see you back."

"Thanks. It's good to be back in the routine."

"The team's all here if you want to say hello."

I'd seen most of them around school today, but not all of them.

"Yeah!" She looked surprised at my excitement, but it was genuine. We'd been through a lot and what we'd worked for had been disrupted.

She moved aside so I could step in the classroom.

"Theo!" Alice jumped up from her desk and came over. She gave me a gentle half hug that kept my left side out of the way.

"Hey."

The rest of the class gathered around.

"Let's give Theo some room," Mrs. H said after there'd been more hugs.

"How are you, Cullen?"

We matched, with slings on opposite arms. His face was bruised. "That dude fucked me over good," he said, shaking his head.

"Cullen!" Mrs. H chastised, but rolled her eyes as well.

"Sorry. There's no better way to describe it." He looked back to me. "I'm working to write with my left hand. The doc says it's unclear if I'll get full usage back on the right."

"Oh, man. I'm sorry."

"Who'd have thought this could go down with a bunch of geeks?" He chuckled, in remarkably good spirits.

"Right. I've never been this hurt in hockey."

We laughed more and some others joined in.

I wanted to ask how they were all doing—really doing, but that seemed awkward. I didn't know these guys that well. I knew they'd all seen counselors, and everyone expected they'd all be resilient. Dean, however, looked off. We needed to catch up one-on-one because we'd been in the thick of it together.

"Theo, I'm actually glad I caught you because I have news." Mrs. H moved in behind her desk. "If you all will take a seat." We quickly settled. "Milestone Security, the company that sponsored the competition, has decided to award all seven schools the prize money."

We broke out into cheers along with some high fives. That'd be so good for the computer-science club.

"In addition," she said, pausing until the cheers died down, "each of you is being awarded an additional twenty-five thousand dollars toward your education. Your parents will get paperwork with details later this week."

Everyone cheered again. Incredible news. I was especially happy about Dean. I suspected this would help a lot. Twenty-five thousand would actually help anyone's education. I wondered if I could give him mine. It wasn't money I expected or really needed. He could make good use of it, though. I'd find a way to make it happen.

Once the excitement settled, I stood. "I should let you guys get on with your meeting. I need to get home. I'm still catching up."

"Hey, Theo." I turned at Jessie's voice. "How'd you stay so calm? You were kinda badass. Dean says you crushed that woman's wrist just like Cullen's and that you saved his life."

I'd hoped that information wouldn't travel too much. Dean knew how to keep secrets. I guess it was inevitable this would come out.

"I didn't know about that." Alice looked pissed.

"Me either," added Cullen.

"I did what I had to," I said, hoping to end this conversation quickly. "I'm sure any of you would've done the same."

"I don't think I know how to crush someone's wrist," Li said.

"Me either, and it happened to me." Cullen held up his arm.

I shrugged. "Well, I did take some self-defense courses over the holidays. After what happened last fall, I wanted to know how to take care of myself."

"We need to let Theo get on his way." Thank God Mrs. H gave me an out.

"I'll see you all around. Please, don't be strangers."

This time I got out of the room and headed for the parking lot.

I was stuck driving. At least I could do that with the sling since most of the important controls for the car were on the right side. I'd figured out early this morning how to hit the turn signal with my right hand while steadying the wheel with my immobilized left.

There were few cars left in the parking lot.

As I got closer to Mom's car, I saw that one of the tires was flat.

"Great," I mumbled.

I had no app for changing a tire. Thankfully we had a AAA membership because there was no way I could do it.

I looked through my contacts to call, and suddenly arms wrapped around me. Pain shot through my shoulder as I was jerked around.

"Hey!" I shouted. I had zero leverage, but despite the pain, I struggled to break the hold. "What the hell?"

"You didn't think we were done, did you, Reese?" Wes came into my field of vision. He snatched my phone and threw it across the parking lot.

He wasted no time punching me in the stomach, sending all the air rushing out of my lungs. I tried to double over, but the person restraining me kept me upright. To make it worse, my restrainer headbutted my shoulder, causing me to yelp from the excruciating pain.

"Does that hurt?" Wes's tone mocked in a singsong fashion. "Let's see how you feel about this."

He stepped closer, and I knew exactly what he planned —knee me liked I'd done to him. I had nowhere to go and did my best to bring my legs together to guard myself.

"People are coming," said the guy who held me. His breath was warm on my neck.

"Yo, Wes. You're not supposed to be here." Dean sounded the most forceful I'd ever heard him. I looked up as Wes glanced back over his shoulder. The entire team, including Mrs. H, ran toward us. Mrs. H was on the phone and following them as fast as she could in her heels.

Wes laughed. "Army of geeks. Whatever." He looked at me. "Hold him tight," he told the guy behind me.

"Seriously? We're outnumbered. And Mrs. H is with them." His cohort didn't release me even as he sounded unsure, but he did release the hold enough to give me room. I quickly moved my right hand to grab my captor's hand so I could spin out of his hold.

Fury etched across Wes's face as he reached for me—a reach I dodged as Dean and Lars got to Wes and held him back. They had a hard time as he bucked and pulled to get away.

"Police are on the way, and Ms. Cohen will be out in a moment," Mrs. H said, grabbing hold of the guy who'd held me and pulling him over near to where Wes was being held.

"Oh come on, Reese and I were working out some stuff from last week." Wes sounded like he was catching on this was trouble for him.

"While you're suspended, being on school property is trespassing so the police are on the way. Not to mention that we all saw what you did." Mrs. H sounded rather satisfied. I guessed her students put up with a lot of crap from the likes of Wes.

Sirens sounded in the distance. "Let me go." Wes sounded defeated as he continued to struggle. The guy who'd held me didn't even try to run for it.

"Oh, Theo," Mrs. H said. She released her grip on Wes's goon and came up to me. "You're bleeding."

Great. With the intensity of the pain, it wasn't surprising that my wound had opened. The stitches weren't due to come out for another few days.

I looked at my shoulder and saw what Mrs. H had. Even through my hoodie and sweatshirt, a splotch of blood had appeared.

Mrs. H looked at me while the police arrived, and Ms. Cohen crossed the parking lot from the other wing of the building.

"I'll put pressure on it." I placed my right hand over the blood spot—almost exactly what I'd done right after I was shot. "There's no way I'm going to easily get out of the clothes to hold it any better."

She nodded. "Probably the best thing. The less movement the better."

The officers arrived, and Mrs. H and the team explained what they'd seen and had them call an ambulance for me. I didn't want another trip to the hospital, but there was no choice. I sat in the back of the police car, holding my shoulder, to wait while the cops talked to people.

"I think you dropped this." Dean held out my phone, with a seriously cracked screen. "You've not had good luck with these the past few days."

"No, I haven't."

We traded easy smiles over the sad state of my phones.

"I didn't get to see you after, but—"

Mrs. H came over. "The ambulance will be here in a minute. They'll take you to Memorial."

I nodded. I needed to call Dad to let him know. I pressed the unlock button on my phone and it didn't respond. Apparently more was wrong than a cracked screen. Lorenzo would start charging for these soon.

"Here." Dean took his from his jeans pocket and handed it to me.

"Thanks."

I made the call. I didn't have to edit anything since this happened at school. He said he and Mom would meet me at the hospital and have John take care of the car. I handed the phone back to Dean.

"So, I haven't really had…. It's not…." Dean paused and seemed to collect himself. "Thank you. I don't know what would've happened if you hadn't been there when they took us to that house."

"Teamwork. I couldn't have done it on my own either."

We looked at each other for a moment. "Actually, I think you could've. Jessie was right, you're pretty badass."

I shrugged, and immediately regretted it.

"Okay, maybe not a complete badass," Dean said through a smirk. "Badasses don't wince when they shrug." He tentatively laughed.

"Jerk." I laughed freely even though that hurt too. At least it hurt less than the shrug.

The ambulance pulled into the parking lot.

"Can we talk one day next week? I've got some afternoons free."

"Uhm… sure." Dean sounded confused.

"Don't worry. It's nothing bad."

"Okay."

"Excuse us. We need to get in here." The paramedics interrupted.

"I'll catch you later," Dean said as he stepped back. Behind the paramedics, I saw Wes and the guy with him being lowered into a police car.

The medics helped me out of the car and to the stretcher. I couldn't hold back a sigh while they loaded me into the ambulance to go to the ER.

Again.

THIRTY-TWO

"Jesus, Theo, I thought I had a lot of hardware. It's like mission control in here." Dean walked around my desk and looked at the monitors, various computers, servers, and other things I had on and behind my desk.

I'd asked him to come over so we could talk privately, and this was the first day we could do it since the whole parking lot incident.

"I admit, some of it's for show, especially the stuff behind the desk. But I use a lot of it. I need powerful stuff for my clients, and for gaming."

"Oh, man. I bet games are sweet with all this processing power and that larger screen."

I dropped my backpack in its usual place by my desk and shrugged out of my coat.

"Wanna give it a go?"

He made a noise that implied I didn't need to ask. "Hell yeah." He took off his jacket and tossed it on the bed.

I brought up the sizable list of games I had on the big screen. "Your pick."

Dean scrolled through the list. It was the most relaxed

I'd ever seen him. Maybe I shouldn't bring up the file, or Wes. Except I wanted to know how he was doing because I'd had similar experiences. Obviously I couldn't discuss Denver, but my abduction was common knowledge.

"Dude, you've got the latest *Grand Theft*. I've been saving for that. Let's do it."

"All right. Gotta warn you, I'm good." I got the game started on the Xbox I had wired in to my hardware.

He grabbed a controller from the bin where I had them stored. "Let's see about that."

After pulling a chair over from the other side of the desk, he plopped himself down next to my chair. I got my controller but stopped short of sitting down.

"Damn. I kinda forgot in the moment." I gestured at my restrained arm and hand.

He shrugged and put the controller on the desk. "It's okay." He tried to cover up his disappointment. "Another time."

"No way." My excitement roared back. "I'll take you with one hand."

He snorted, which made me even more determined. I gently adjusted my arm in the sling, taking the thumb out of its restraint. Locking the controller into my left hand, I settled into a position that seemed like it would work. It'd be awkward, but testing things out, I could make do.

"You sure about this?" Dean took up his controller. "I don't want to be responsible for breaking you worse."

"You can try." I was just as cocky with him as I was with Eddie and Mitch.

"Let's do this."

We dropped into the game. It wasn't easy with one hand, and there were times I pulled on my shoulder, but it was fun. Dean had an interesting strategy, and it made me think a little more than usual too. He seemed to be into the game, really moving his chair as he played.

Suddenly he hit the pause button, but he didn't take his eyes off the screen.

He was silent for a moment. "How did you not freak out?" His gaze stayed focused on the frozen game.

"I was terrified, but I couldn't let her scare everyone else," I said quietly, lying because I wasn't *that* terrified. "I did what had to be done. Same as you."

"I didn't have a choice. I...." He finally looked at me and sighed. "If I'd said no, it would've been so much worse."

"But you didn't."

I wanted to do something. He looked so uncomfortable. "You saved my life. I don't know what to say to that. I've thought about it—a lot. Thank you seems too little." More silence, but he still looked at me. "I don't know."

He looked away again and rubbed his hand over his slightly scruffy cheek.

"You would've done the same."

"I hope so. But I honestly don't know. Sometimes terror paralyzed me, even trying to get the machine to blow up. There are blank spots. Things I don't remember."

Hopefully I was going to say the right thing. "You know I got snatched off my bike last fall?"

He nodded.

"That was terrifying. Guys in masks, with guns. Why were they after me? I didn't know what to do. But then Eddie showed up because I'd called him and told him something felt off. He risked himself for me. And I found the courage to use his distraction to get away. You did what you had to do to get out of the situation."

He fidgeted with the controller, and it seemed like he was going to speak, but he didn't.

"You have no idea how scared I was to be shoved into that van. I think I'll always have a thing against vans," I continued. "Are you talking to anyone about all this?"

"Yeah, the school's got me a counselor to talk to and Mom's making me go. Don't you have to do it too? I thought the whole team had to do it."

I smiled. "I already was. Since the abduction I've been seeing someone. This is just one more thing for us to talk about. It helps to talk it out with someone who wasn't involved."

"I see bits of it when I go to sleep. Sometimes it doesn't end like it did."

I nodded. "I know."

"Who'd have thought that competition could end so messed up."

"Right? At least we ended up with the prize—it was cool of the sponsor to do that."

"Yeah. They did right by everybody. It'll help me get to college for sure."

I paused. I'd rehearsed this in my head most of the day, but I didn't want him to get pissed off.

"I've talked to my advisor at MIT, told him about the skills I've seen and that I think you'd be great for the program. He'd love to meet you."

He broke out in a laugh. "Even with the prize money, I could never afford MIT. My grades aren't good enough and that means no scholarship." The laugh abruptly stopped. "Plus my family could really use some of that money. I appreciate what you tried to do, but I think I'd waste his time. I'm looking at Roxbury. They've got Information Science courses. It's about all I can afford. If I can get my grades up, maybe I can get a scholarship later."

"If there's anything I can do to help...."

He nodded.

"Get back to the game?" I gestured at the frozen screen that waited in front of us. I didn't want to push him any more than I already had.

"Yeah." He turned back to the screen, but then looked at me. "Ready?"

I got positioned to play again and gave a curt nod. He clicked the pause button and we were playing again.

THIRTY-THREE

BIZARRE.

That was the most accurate description for it. I'd never watched a McKinley game from the stands. I'd hated watching the Denver championship game last fall with my parents and Eddie, and this was about a zillion times worse. I hadn't known the Denver team well because it'd been thrown together the day before the tourney began.

My team was playing, and I should be out there with them. In the few times I'd missed school games, I hadn't come to watch. Last week it'd been easy to skip because it was an away game and I'd only been out of the hospital a couple of days. Tonight we were playing at home, and I wanted to show my support. It might've been a mistake. Even though the Tigers were winning, it gnawed at me that I couldn't contribute for my teammates. I did my best not to show my disappointment as I yelled and cheered with Iris and Eddie.

Coach Daly tried to simplify everything—do the rehabilitation and get a full season for my senior year. He then put it all into perspective, telling me to be proud that I'd likely averted a national catastrophe and shouldn't sweat a few games.

He was right.

It didn't change my unhappiness on the sidelines, especially since it was where I'd be for several weeks.

Eddie put his hand on my knee and brought my attention back to the rink.

"You okay?" He looked concerned.

"Yeah. Why?" I hoped to play off the fact I'd been too in my head.

"You missed Mitch scoring."

"Shit. Sorry. I was busy beating myself up."

He nodded and gave me a slight smile.

"Please don't say 'It's not your fault, Theo.'"

"Oh, I wouldn't say that." Eddie was in a ridiculously good mood, and with the teasing tone he used, I was eager to hear what else he had to say.

"Really?"

"Not at all. It's totally your fault." On the other side of Eddie, Iris shot him a shocked look he couldn't see since he faced me. "You got involved in the very dangerous sport of computer-science competitions, and you've paid the price."

Eddie said it so earnestly that I chuckled.

"Edward Cochrane, what a horrible thing to say!" Iris slapped his shoulder several times, and the chuckles escalated into big laughs.

And then it was hysterics I couldn't control.

I hadn't busted out this hard in a while, and it felt great. The movement irritated my shoulder, but it didn't matter. Iris looked at me like I'd gone mad, and that only made me laugh more. Eddie, however, smiled—a truly sweet smile.

He'd just done more for my mood than anything else had in days. It didn't matter that people around us turned to see what was so funny; I relished the moment.

As my laughter died out, I leaned into Eddie so my head rested against his shoulder. "You're awesome."

"You might need to tell Iris that." He kissed the side of my head. "I'm glad it didn't backfire."

"I loved it and I needed it."

The second period ended about five minutes after Mitch's goal, and we led three to two.

"How about some hot chocolate?" I sat up and looked at Eddie.

"And maybe one of those snickerdoodles if they have any?"

"Oh yeah." We stood up, but Iris stayed seated. "Want to come?"

"Nah." She smiled at us. "You two go on. Bring me back a coffee, though?"

"Will do," Eddie said.

We made our way out of the aisle, down the stairs, and out into the lobby. People seemed to have burned out their questions. When Eddie and I had arrived, a lot of parents asked how I was, if I'd play again this season, and so on. It'd only been a few days since the questions stopped at school, and I wasn't prepared to face them all over again. That's probably what sent me into the funk.

"Thanks for that." I held Eddie's hand while we stood in the concession line.

"Anytime. I was surprised you drifted away. You've seemed to be managing okay."

"It really hit me hard being a spectator and that I'm not going to be out there again for weeks. I've tried to focus more on the idea that this," I said, pointing at my sling, "got us more time together—and that's never a bad thing."

"I like when you talk about more time together."

My phone vibrated in a TOS pattern. The phone was in my right pocket, which bumped up against Eddie's leg, so he felt it too.

Eddie squeezed my hand, and I knew it was a plea to ignore the phone. It stopped, having gone to voicemail. It was difficult to not pull away to check it, but I didn't. It hadn't been a priority ring.

"Can we skip the team party and do something else? Just us?" I asked. "Maybe go to the café and chill?"

"My parents are at some... I don't know what... but shouldn't be home until around midnight."

"Why are we even here, then?"

Eddie laughed. "It's what we do. Cheer for our friends."

I smiled. "That we do."

After we paid and were waiting for our order, I took the moment to get my phone and see who'd called.

"I knew you wouldn't be able to keep away from that too long," Eddie said, his disappointment crystal clear.

"It'll just take a second."

"You say that, and then you disappear for hours."

I stayed next to him to show I wasn't going anywhere. I read an email from the person who called. It was an analysis on the attack on my phone that happened at Eddie's swim meet along with the virus from Eddie's thumb drive. Two documents were attached. She'd been busy. She said she could walk me through the findings when I was ready. That could wait until morning.

"See. I'm already done." I pocketed the phone when our order came up.

His expression remained clouded, troubled. He had more to say.

"I'm sorry," I said softly.

"I know." He picked up the cookies and put them in his jacket pocket. I took my hot chocolate while he took his and Iris's coffee. "You've got responsibilities. I knew that when we started going out. More keeps piling on, though." He looked at me and gestured over to an empty table. "There's only so much time in a day, and it feels like the amount of time there is for us gets less and less."

The words hurt more than the bullet had. Unfortunately he wasn't wrong. He usually got the leftovers on my schedule. It wasn't fair. Mom and Dad always wanted to make sure I was having a life, and being a teenager. I manage everything pretty well, except the guy I love.

"You're right." I fought the urge to look away. "I need to reprioritize."

"I'd like that. But I'm not sure it's fair for me to ask you to do it."

With my good hand, I lifted one of his hands from his cup and held it.

"You're not asking. I'm saying it. I want more time with you, and it's up to me to make the time. My injury gives us some." I held his gaze. "I'm going to create more time for us."

"You building some sort of time machine?" A slight smile appeared.

"I wish."

"If anyone could, I'd put my money on you." He moved our hands so he could squeeze mine. "Theo, I love you and I know you love me. But I don't know.... It feels like we're thirty and dealing with the real world instead of being high school juniors and supposedly having it a little easier." I didn't like where it sounded like he was headed. "You're crazy talented. I can't ask you to stop. I know it's work, but you enjoy it—at least most of the time I think you do." He sighed. "I need to focus on the time we get and not bitch so much about the rest."

I quietly released the breath I'd been holding. I didn't want to break up with him.

"Yes, I love you," I said, holding his gaze. "I'm crazy for you. I need to hold back less. I need to tell you when work's going crazy and you need to tell me when you're feeling ignored."

"I'm sorry I was—"

"No. Don't apologize." I looked at the cups in front of us. "What do you say we take Iris her coffee and then duck out of here?"

"Are you sure? I know you want to support the team. If I was injured, I'd want to be there for my guys. It's only another half hour or so."

He knew me so well. I wanted to leave, but here was important too.

"Let's get back in there, then," he said.

We picked up the drinks and returned to our seats. The Tigers delivered a four to three win, and we cheered loudly in the third period as Skyler, our goalie, stood on his head to keep the opponent from scoring during their end-of-game onslaught seeking a tie.

Iris sent us on our way after the game. She said if Mitch had issues because we left, she'd give him hell for it. I had no doubt she would, but I knew Mitch would understand.

It didn't take long for us to pull up in front of Eddie's house in his Jeep. The house was dark. We hopped out, and he grabbed my hand when I came around the front and met up with him.

"The stars are amazing." He gestured, with his head, up to the sky. "It's like super clear tonight. Wish it was warmer so we could stay outside, settle into the hammock in the backyard or something."

"I'm game if you are." I knew he tended to be colder than me. I think being on the ice so much upped my tolerance for cold, as opposed to his time in heated pools.

His look said I might be crazy, but he nodded and then broke into a grin. "Come on."

When we entered the house, my watch pulsed, but since Eddie held my hand, I couldn't easily take a look. Why would one of my alarms be going off here? Eddie didn't have tech that would do that. I'd examined what was here once, and it was basic consumer stuff. I even made sure to recheck every few months because I came over so often. It had to be a glitch. Maybe something didn't transfer into my new phone right.

"I'm gonna run up and grab the blanket from my bed. Be right back." We shared a quick kiss.

The watch continued to pulse every few seconds, and the word *icing* showed on the face. Just like when Dean tried and that time after the swim meet. I pulled my phone and dismissed the message from the home screen. I debated powering it off, but I couldn't. I had to be mostly available.

Looking at the security log, I found something pinging the phone from an unknown source. The IP wasn't one I recognized from the local cable company. I flipped over to a security app I'd designed with TOS and set it to isolate what was coming from the signal. The app would quarantine what it received, run some limited analysis, and send logs to the TOS repository for further study. It could be nothing more than someone screwing around to see what they could find. It didn't seem directed at my device specifically.

"Take this outside and get yourself comfortable. I'm gonna get the heater from the garage. It'll give us a little bit of warmth."

"Hang on a second. Can I see your phone?"

He wrinkled his brow at my non sequitur, but pulled it from his pocket, unlocked it with his thumb, and handed it over. "What's up?"

"The security on my phone went off when we walked in. I want to see if your phone is affected too."

"Um, okay." He shook his head but smiled. "Sometimes I think you might be too smart for your own good. I'll be back in a second." He laid the blanket over the stair rail before he darted to the garage.

I used my phone to examine his. No surprise that he was on the Wi-Fi, which was unimaginatively named by his father as *Cochrane Family*. I'd encouraged them to not make it so obvious, but at least they kept it secure. I was on the public cell network. Moving quickly, I established that Eddie's phone was receiving the same signal. Like mine, his phone didn't seem adversely affected, so I did a quick adjustment to block the signal.

"Everything okay?" Eddie held the small black heater in his hand along with an extension cord.

"I guess." I handed his phone back. "I blocked it from your phone and...." My watch pulsed, and I looked to find the all-clear message. "Well, whatever it was is gone." The security app scans showed nothing. "I saved some details that I can analyze and see if I can figure out what it was. Let's go."

I grabbed the blanket and headed through the house to the sliding glass door in the living room. We went outside, and Eddie paused for a moment to plug in the cord. At the hammock, which was stretched across a metal frame, he put the heater on the adjacent table.

I got in first and moved far to the left to keep my shoulder protected, and then he climbed in. We'd been in this hammock enough that we didn't have to jostle to find the right positions; we fit easily together and my injury didn't change that. It was weird being in so many clothes, though. We usually only did this in the summer when we were in T-shirts and shorts—and sometimes just shorts.

The mix of the chilled night air, with the heat that blew across us, made a cozy environment. We leaned toward each other. Normally we'd hold each other closer, but even with my left arm restrained—and jammed between us—we still managed to make it so we could kiss. Eddie stabilized me by having his hand at my waist. I ached to hug him, but was still more than satisfied with the closeness.

As was usually the case, we could only stay this way for fifteen or twenty minutes before the arms we trapped under us were prickly from being put to sleep. With a grunt from me, we broke the kisses and moved into our other standard position—Eddie's arm extended behind me to allow me to use his chest as a pillow. I was still sort of on my side, but the pressure was off my right arm, and I snuggled up next to him in one of my favorite positions.

"This is perfect," Eddie said quietly, like he might be worried he'd disturb the atmosphere we'd created.

I gave a contented sigh. "Yeah."

"Ooh. I can make it more perfect." Eddie shifted gently and dug into his jacket pocket.

"Yes! I forgot you had those."

"Got 'em." He pulled the bag of cookies out and held it aloft. He seemed unsure how to proceed.

"Use my arm for something." The sling held my arm close to my body and made my arm a pretty decent ledge the way we were positioned. It was the best option since he only had one arm free.

It worked perfectly, if you didn't count the crumbs that fell between us. He gave me a bite of cookie before he took a bite too.

"It's awkward, but it works if you don't move and knock the other cookie off."

"I think I can manage." I smiled as he took another bite.

It was usually before or after a make-out session that we snuggled. If we watched TV, we were usually sitting up, albeit close. Eddie'd mentioned that our relationship some-times felt like we were adults. I wasn't sure this was an adult thing, but this was a flash-forward on our future—cuddled up, enjoying each other's company, either talking or in silence, with the shared connection that a couple has. Mom and Dad did this sometimes, probably not often enough. I'd see them together on a couch, maybe reading or chatting. I wanted that, and I enjoyed this glimpse of what we could be doing in a few years.

"You okay?" I hadn't realized I'd drifted away until he spoke. I bit off some cookie he offered and chewed as I nodded.

"Yeah," I finally said. "It'd be nice to end days like this more often. Maybe we move in together when we go to college?"

I'm not sure I meant to say that. It might've been too much, but it was out there now.

"That'd be cool." Eddie didn't miss a beat. "Do you worry that we'd never get anything done because we'd always be like this?"

I chuckled. "We'd sure *want* to be like this."

"For sure."

We munched on the cookies, made out, and stayed snuggled until close to midnight. Leaving sucked, but this wasn't our reality yet. It sure seemed like it could be, though.

THIRTY-FOUR

SATURDAY, two weeks after the competition, I was back at TOS headquarters. Dad came along this time to take care of some business. I dressed less formally this time with a sport coat over a T-shirt. Lorenzo wore this a lot and it fit my style more than a dress shirt and tie. My slinged arm was under the jacket so that I could easily remove the top layer if I wanted.

It was difficult to be gone for part of another weekend. Eddie's swim meet was under way. At least Mitch and Iris were there to make sure the team had support. Eddie was disappointed that Dad was taking me to see his parents—a good cover story since they lived only a couple of hours from Boston. Luckily Eddie had perked up when I said it was only a day trip, and I'd be back in time to see him tonight.

I'd spent the morning with Raptor, TOS's director, and Joanna to debrief further on what had gone down at the competition. Granted, I could've done the meetings on video chat, but I also wanted to see Lorenzo in person. With my injury, we'd delayed my transition to taking over portions of Keys's duties. However, those days had given me more time to think.

Every time I thought about having a staff, even one I wouldn't be responsible for sending out in the field, I got butterflies. The more I tried to tell myself it would be okay, the more the butterflies swarmed. I'd guided the computer-science team, and that didn't turn out too bad, at least in terms of the actual objectives of the competition.

I'd talked to Mom, Dad, and Shields about the causalities and injuries. In particular I was disturbed that I wasn't feeling too bad about them. It was sad that Chet died and that Cullen's wrist was badly damaged, but neither incident weighed on me as much as I thought it should.

All of them essentially gave the same advice: Over time you learn that you can't take responsibility for what you can't control. You can still have empathy for the situation, and help the people involved, but you have to give yourself permission to not let it eat you up inside.

It some ways it seemed cold, especially on first consideration. But it didn't take long for it to make sense. If you beat yourself up too much over what you can't control, it's a sure way to burn out or worse.

Lorenzo's door was open when I arrived so I knocked on the frame. He looked over from the screen he was reading. He smiled, more broadly than I'd seen in a few days, but it disappeared when I didn't return one.

"Uh-oh, was the debrief okay?" he asked, turning his chair so he directly faced me. "Have a seat."

I entered and closed the door since this needed to be private. I dropped into one of the chairs across from him. The butterflies were awful, worse than when I'd been here for Keys's wake. I shouldn't be nervous talking to Lorenzo about anything, but this time out I thought the nerves might make me throw up. I tried to keep the anxiety contained so he wouldn't catch on. So far, I wasn't doing a great job with managing my mood.

"Yeah, the meeting was good. Recapped everything I knew and discussed Dean's part in depth because they were curious about him. They're actually going to try to get him more college funds so he can get into a better school, which is great. They were pleased with how I managed everything."

"Of course they were," Lorenzo said. He was obviously trying to get me to be more upbeat. But the longer I sat here the more my insides were going crazy. "What aren't you telling me? There's nothing—"

"I don't think I can take the promotion." The words spilled out of my mouth so fast. It was like opening a shaken soda can.

His expression stayed calm with no trace of disappointment or anger.

"Or, rather, I don't think I should take it," I said quietly.

He nodded slowly.

"I'm sorry I said yes in the first place," I said, wanting him to have the whole story. "I'm really honored you think I can do the job. And I think I'd do okay, but it's not the right time. You need someone who can be available, and not just for the duration of a mission, but always a phone call away. That's not possible for me right now. The more I thought about it, especially after this"—I gently gestured with my slinged arm—"along with the fact that, well, I think I need time to...."

"Be a kid?" he asked tentatively.

I sighed because part of me hated admitting this. "Yeah."

"Theo, it's okay to admit that. You've got a lot of skills,

but you are still a teenager. This isn't TV—like Doogie Howser or Sheldon Cooper where the boy geniuses are out of college and working. It was wrong of me to even ask."

Tension in my shoulders and chest relaxed, like a rubber band being gently released. "I'm still really thankful you thought enough of me to want me to do it."

"Still." He shook his head. "I told you before that it's so easy to forget how old you are. Looking back, I was too eager to get someone into the job, and you've got all the technical qualifications. I had no reservations about asking you. I think my enthusiasm for bringing you into it clouded Joanna's judgment too. She did ask a couple of times if I thought it was completely the right choice, and I kept saying yes."

"Thanks for not being mad," I said along with a small smile.

"I'm not." He leaned forward and locked his gaze on mine. "*This* is the right choice. I was actually trying to figure out how to ask you one more time if you were sure you wanted the job. I didn't want to take it back, but the idea of you burning out crossed my mind more than once. That's the last thing I'd want. Plus, your parents would come after me if I let that happen, and I do not want on their bad side."

He raised his eyebrows and made a hint of a smile. It was a perfect move and helped prove that he was okay even while I struggled with expectations of myself.

"Why would you be worried about Mom and Dad?" I tried to move the conversation elsewhere.

"I know what they're capable of. The last thing I'd want is for that to be unleashed on me."

I knew too. I'd helped on enough of their missions to know you didn't mess with them.

"I'll still consult on anything you need in addition to my regular assignments."

He nodded. "Look, we've worked together long enough that you've got nothing to prove to me. I can see you're beating yourself up over turning this down."

I nodded. "And you know how to read me too." I gave a nervous laugh. "For what it's worth, I'm talking to Shields about the expectations I set for myself. She's used the word burnout with me too."

"Good. I want you around here for a good long time."

"What do we do about the team meeting?" I asked. We were supposed to meet with Keys's former team today to talk about me coming in.

"We'll let them know about the change of plan, take questions, and move on from there. I'm not worried and you shouldn't be either. You're a respected part of the team, and you're recovering from field work. This will be fine."

We left his office and headed for the conference room. The butterflies were back with a vengeance. Lorenzo had been okay with my choice, but what would the team think of the change of plan?

The team was already gathered and mostly standing and chatting with each other. It wasn't completely a stereotypical meeting of computer geeks. Sure there were a lot of black T-shirts, hoodies, and glasses, but there were many colorful personal style choices.

Along the sides of the room, monitors were set up to display staff that were either deployed on assignment or simply couldn't get here. In all there were twelve on the team, and only one was missing due to an assignment in progress.

Lorenzo took the chair at the head of the table and indicated an adjacent open chair for me. The staff immediately settled as we sat.

"Thank you all for taking a few minutes to gather, especially on a Saturday," Lorenzo said. "We've had a change of plan. After some reconsideration, I've decided to fully manage the team for now. While Theo has the skills"—he gestured my way—"tasking someone who is still in high school with the responsibilities was probably not my best idea. We want Theo to complete high school and college successfully so he'll be ready to give his full attention to his work here."

Holy crap. I didn't expect him to take the full responsibility for the change. Since it was my choice I was willing to own that to this team. Still, it was great he was doing this. I decided to not speak up since it wouldn't look good for either of us to contradict him.

"Joanna and I will be looking for candidates to fill this role," Lorenzo continued. "In the meantime, I'll continue to lead and rely on each of you to keep current projects moving and to speak up if you see anything that needs attention. Are there any questions about this change or anything else?"

"Theo, how's your shoulder?" Jenna asked from the opposite end of the table.

I chuckled. "Pretty useless. Working with only one hand isn't easy. Unfortunately I had a scuffle at school last week and it pulled the wound open, so that was a setback."

She nodded. "The amount of typing we do, I can't imagine having to do it with one hand. I hope it heals up soon."

"Me too." I smiled back at her. "It has been a good opportunity to work with some voice recognition tech, though. There could be some interesting applications for us that I might have some ideas for."

"Sorry I couldn't be there in person," Marcus said from one of the monitors. "If I missed my daughter's soccer game, I'd be in trouble with her. I've got one question."

"Of course, Marcus. What is it?" Lorenzo responded.

"Theo's been in the field twice now and Keys... well, she died in the field. Do you think we're going to end up out there more?"

"Field work will continue to be on an as-needed basis. We are, however, putting together additional training to better equip us mentally and physically when we're deployed. It won't be full field training, but it'll be more rigorous that what we currently have. That'll be rolling out by summer."

The new training was something Lorenzo, Joanna, and I talked about, both after Denver and in my debriefs from what just happened. I know what I'd learned from John and Coach helped me, so it made sense to expand everyone's skill set since the IT team only had the most basic training. While that was renewed every six months, IT did not receive the more advanced courses Mom, Dad, and true field agents received.

"Great. That'll be good to have so we're all prepared for anything that comes up."

Lorenzo nodded. "I hope Lila's team wins."

"Thanks," Marcus said.

"Anything else?" Lorenzo scanned the room. "No?" He waited for another moment. "Okay. That was easy. I'll let you get back to whatever you've got going on today. Thanks everyone."

People began filing out, and some of them stopped to offer me congratulations on the mission along with good thoughts on my shoulder.

"Dean did quite a number on that machine," Lorenzo said once we were alone. "I just skimmed the report that came in. It seems he exploited a few hardware and firmware holes to make it self-destruct."

"It looked pretty spectacular in person. I shouldn't have been surprised by it based on what I've seen him do over the past couple weeks between his attempt to get into my phone, putting Wes through hell, and his work in class."

"Is he as good as you?"

"Possibly. There hasn't been a chance for a true head-to-head match. He poked at my phone, but didn't get in. It's possible, I suppose, given time that he could." I quickly scanned the report. "They recovered file fragments and they're *reasonably* confident it's the original?"

"Yeah. I don't like the reasonably part. You saw the data when it opened and there was no error message like the first time. But there was certainly a hole in the initial security that allowed the stolen laptop to be compromised to allow the file to be moved. It's not clear if Coyle managed to make viable copies. We've found an array of hacks that were in progress, and all of those revealed a copied file with the same error you saw. Other agencies have intercepted copies as well."

I nodded. "We should leave the bots in place to keep watch for anything, even copies."

"Agreed."

"Hey guys." Dad stood in the doorway of the conference room.

"Victor, good to see you." Lorenzo stood and shook Dad's hand. "You guys headed out?"

"Only if you two are finished."

Lorenzo and I looked at each other and he nodded. "I think we are."

"Thank you," I said, holding his gaze. "You took the

total hit for the last-minute change. You didn't have to do that. I was ready to own it."

"I put you in that position, though, so the fault was on me." Lorenzo was about to clap me on the shoulder, but stopped even though it was my good one. "Fist-bump instead." And we did, both grinning. "Now get out of here. Hopefully we won't talk again until Monday when we should be back talking about souped up contact lenses instead of stolen encrypted keys."

"Sounds good. See you both later." Lorenzo departed.

"Contact lenses?" Dad asked, an eyebrow raised.

"Yeah," I said excitedly. "Think Geordi on *Next Gen*."

"Really?"

"If we can get the bugs worked out, yeah."

"I've no doubt you will. The tech team is always working miracles." I left the conference room ahead of Dad, and we walked side by side through the corridor. "Let's get out of here. *Mr. Robot* is waiting on the plane."

I grinned. Our *Mr. Robot* viewing had been delayed by more than a few days, but the travel time was the perfect chance to get a couple of episodes knocked off our list.

ACKNOWLEDGEMENTS

I'm thrilled to bring Theo's second mission to the page. He's tremendously fun to write, and I hope you enjoy reading this adventure that keeps him closer to home this time out.

Thanks to my friends who read early versions of *Schooled* to make sure it worked: Brian, Chris, David, Elvis, and Michael. Having their input was so valuable as I worked my way to a final story. Additional gratitude goes to Dawn, Laura, Victoria, and Liz. I appreciate the time you each spent with the story and your great suggestions to improve it.

And, as always, thanks to Will for all of his love and support.

MISSION PREVIEW

AUDIO ASSAULT

CODENAME: WINGER #3

MISSION PREVIEW: AUDIO ASSAULT
CHAPTER ONE

"*Winger, Amp here. My position's about to be compromised. I'm not sure how much longer I can stay here.*"

Through the comm channel, tension dripped from the agent's quiet voice. Twenty-three years old and new to Tactical Operational Support, Amp sounded green and unsure. Reminded me of my first field mission less than a year ago.

"Hang tight, Amp. Focus on the neutralization of the firewall." I projected calm because it's what my team needed. Meanwhile, from an electrical equipment closet on the first floor, I worked to take over the research facility's security system so it would appear as though multiple breaches were in progress. "Petty, do you have eyes on Amp's position?"

"*There are three working to open the door where Amp is.*" Petty didn't have a tremble in her voice even though this was her first time too. No doubt part of that was her safer position in the van outside. "*They've brought in a blowtorch to get through the door.*"

"*Winger, what am I going to do?*"

"You keep working. You're there because you know what needs to be done. We'll keep you safe."

The building's security was ridiculous in its complexity. Usually it was easy to find the logic in a system, this one seemed to have none. Maybe that was the point. I hoped to use the intricacies to force its downfall.

"Petty, how many inside?"

"Stand by."

As the seconds ticked by, I got fidgety. "Petty?"

"Winger, one moment."

"Don't have a moment, Petty." Annoyance slipped into my voice, which I didn't like. Petty and Amp were assigned to me for this mission, and it fell to me to be senior agent in charge.

"Winger, they're cutting through. There's already a small hole in the door. I need at least another two minutes."

"Understood, Amp." He was right on schedule. In the mission briefing, he said he'd need fifteen minutes, and he was at thirteen. "Petty, now."

"Seventeen across the three floors. Biggest clusters are on three and one."

Time to make a distraction. I sent commands to deceive the security system into thinking an intruder breached a second-floor lab.

"Petty, disable the monitors on my mark but maintain your visibility."

"Understood. Standing by."

After a double-check of the commands, I poised my finger over the enter key. "Now, Petty."

"Monitors disabled."

"Distraction enabled." The security statuses flipped from green to red on the south side of the second floor.

"No one's moving to that area, Winger."

"What?"

"*Confirmed.*" Petty continued. "*They're ignoring it.*"

What the hell? My monitor returned to green status. Everything seemed in order to make this work, especially since I saw—There was a loop of logic checks. This design was clever. I read quickly through the code and found the subroutine causing the problem.

"Stand by."

We got bad intel on this place. No mention of buried security measures appeared in any of the reports. If we'd known that, we wouldn't have sent Amp in before we knew we had control. I shouldn't have sent him to start before I confirmed we could keep him safe. Now we needed an improvised distraction or he'd be exposed and the mission would fail.

I typed rapidly, looking for a way to make the security sensors trip.

"Petty, keep me posted on Amp's status."

"*Copy that, Winger.*"

Nothing worked. Apparently only the door sensor could send the right command back to central control to confirm an intruder. There was no time to figure this out.

"*Damnit. Winger, I need more time. I've run into interference. Someone's trying to kick me out. My timeline is shot.*"

"Understood, Amp. Petty, do you have eyes on me?"

"*Confirmed, Winger.*"

This sucked hard, but there was little choice. If I couldn't make a distraction remotely, I'd have to do it manually.

"Amp, I'm en route to your location. Keep at it and stop for nothing."

"*But—*"

"Understood?"

Silence filled the channel for a moment. *"Copy that."* He clearly didn't like it.

"Petty, help me stay out of sight."

"Got it."

"You're clear for the corridor you're in and then on to the elevators and stairs."

"Understood."

Despite the info, I opened the door slowly and peeked around the corner. Since it was after hours, the lighting was at half, but that wouldn't obscure me if anyone came into the hall.

Amp was on the second floor, but I wanted a distraction down here to draw people in this direction. The windows would be a good target if I could disrupt those sensors. I pulled my phone as I got to the stairs and brought up the building schematics. I needed to know where the sensors were.

"Winger," Petty said. *"Guards leaving the lobby. Get out of the hall."*

I opened the stairway door slowly to avoid noise and ducked in. There was no window in the door so I couldn't see once it closed.

"Stand by. They're past you but not out of the hall."

All the doors and windows had sensors. I looked around the perimeter of the stairwell door and found one along the top.

Damn. No wires ran to the small block so severing the connection couldn't happen. There was no time to figure out how to disrupt the wireless network that linked the sensors.

New plan.

I considered my options as I sprinted upstairs.

"Petty, tell me about the third floor."

"Two guards are at the elevator bank behind a desk. Another is on patrol. Exit the staircase, go right and then left, and you'll be out of sight for a few moments. But you've got to move now."

I moved quick, happy I kept up with endurance exercises during the hockey off-season. At the door, I asked, "Clear?"

"Clear."

I ended up in a hall filled with doors locked by retinal-scan and card-access readers. This should do the trick.

"Amp here. I think I've got less than five minutes before they're in here. There's even more resistance in the network. They're tag-teaming me. I could really use you in here, Winger."

"Here comes the distraction."

I stepped up to the first scanner and pushed the only available button. Bright light hit my eye and the scanner turned red.

"Unauthorized," a mechanical female voice announced.

Finally.

I moved to the next door and did it again.

"Three guards are headed your way."

I moved to the other scanners quickly. The more alerts the better.

"Petty, next stairwell?"

"Three doors down on your left. You've got maybe fifteen seconds before they'll see you."

I ignored other sensors and made for the staircase.

"Where am I going to come out on two?" I asked as I headed down.

Another set of labs, bigger. Only two on the corridor. The guards are checking the doors on three, but one is headed into the stairway, and he's on his radio.

"Which way do I go to get to Amp?"

"Out of the staircase, go right. That's clear. Finding the best route from there."

"Copy that."

I followed the instructions and pressed my eye into the sensors at the labs I passed.

"You don't have time for that. Take the next right and then look sharp. There are a lot of intersections. You're going to take the third left, and you'll be in the corridor where Amp is. He's still got one person on his door. The other guards have dispersed, most are on three."

I jogged down the hall with a stop to scan my unauthorized eye. Unexpectedly the hall lights went red and klaxons sounded.

That was new. Even though I didn't know what caused it, I appreciated the extra noise to bring attention here.

"Amp's door is clear. The guard's coming your way. Two more from behind. Get to the last intersection and go left. That's the clearest bet, and you'll get back to Amp."

This was more fun than it should be. Sure, bad guys were coming, but running around in the corridors was an ultimate game of laser tag. I desperately did not want to get tagged.

"Winger, I'm in." I smiled at the thrill in Amp's voice. "Beginning data transfer."

"Excellent. I'm on my way. Less than a minute."

"You need to hurry, Winger. The guards are all responding to the last alarm you triggered. Take the next right. Amp is two doors from the end of the corridor. They'll cut you off if you don't hurry."

I didn't have much speed to add, but I pushed.

"The guy's back working with the door." Petty broke the news just as I turned into the hallway. We were both dressed in black. Maybe he'd mistake me for security as well.

"He's almost through the entire frame." To his credit, Amp sounded calmer.

I slowed. The man at the door needed to believe I was part of his team.

"Winger, you're about to get pinned if the guard in the staircase to your left enters the floor."

There was nowhere for me to go.

"Amp," I was very quiet, knowing the comms would still pick up my voice, "no matter what finish the mission and make sure you get all the data."

There was only a short pause. *"Understood."*

I heard the stairway open behind me and boots on the floor.

"You there," barked a new voice, "identify yourself."

"Security. Hauer." I didn't turn or break stride.

He's closing on you, Winger.

The loud clomps made that obvious. He must not have a stealth mode. The dude at the door turned his attention to me.

"Amp, can you help Winger?"

"No. The download is too unstable."

"Where's your badge?" asked the guy who'd been cutting the door open. A badge clipped to the front of his shirt hung over the pocket. He dropped his hand to the holster at his waist.

"Oh, man. Sorry. I forgot to clip it on when I started my shift." Fishing around in my pockets, I had to buy a few more seconds.

"I've never heard of a Hauer," said the man behind me.

He shoved me forward as the guy in front of me aimed his gun. "Get your hands out of your pockets."

When I didn't immediately comply, he grabbed my right hand to forcibly remove it.

"Who are you? How'd you get in here?" Another shove from behind sent me sideways into the wall.

"I'll have to talk to HR if you keep touching me." I shrugged him off as he grabbed for me. "I told you I've got a badge. I just need to get it."

"Winger, what are you doing?" Petty sounded nervous.

"Let me help you." The man was in my face and he dug into my left pocket but came up with nothing. From my right, he pulled out my phone. "He's got no ID." He threw the phone to the floor.

"Now, who are you?" The man with the gun asked as he moved closer.

"Hey, Siri. Pulse."

"Opening app Pulse," Siri said.

"What did you do?"

"Five...." A male voice came from the phone.

"Turn it off." The man with the gun twitched as the other guard picked up the phone.

"Four...."

He pulled the gun's hammer back. "Now."

"Three...."

"Hey, Siri. Stop Pulse!" the guard clutched the phone, screaming at it.

Did he really think it would take commands from anyone but me?

"Two...."

"Stop it!" the gunman shouted at me, but I only shook my head. "Smash it!"

The guy holding the phone threw it down and stomped on it with his heel.

"One...." Despite the crunch of the screen's glass, it kept going.

The gun fired.

The impact slammed my chest.

"Pulse."

Sparks flew from the lights and door mechanisms as well as the guard's pockets.

I clutched my chest where the bullet hit.

"Winger!" Amp and Petty shouted into my ear.

Pain radiated from my chest as I crumpled to the floor.

Both guards shook, and one cried out, as they fell.

"Get that data secured," I called out as red spilled out between my fingers.

Winger's missions continue with *Audio Assault*
Available in ebook, paperback and audiobook

This excerpt is Copyright © 2018 by Jeff Adams

YOUNG ADULT BOOKS BY JEFF ADAMS

Each of these titles are available in ebook, paperback and audiobook

Codename: Winger series

Tracker Hacker (includes the bonus short story *A Very Winger Christmas*)

Schooled

Audio Assault

Netminder

Other Young Adult Titles

Flipping for Him

ABOUT THE AUTHOR

Jeff Adams has written stories since he was in middle school and became a published author in 2009 when his first short stories were published. He writes both gay romance and LGBTQ+ young adult fiction...and there's usually a hockey player at the center of the story.

Jeff lives in central California with his husband of more than twenty years, Will. Some of his favorite things include the musicals *Rent* and *[title of show],* the Detroit Red Wings and Pittsburgh Penguins hockey teams, and the reality TV competition *So You Think You Can Dance.* He, of course, loves to read, but there isn't enough space to list out his favorite books.

Jeff and Will are also podcasters. The *Big Gay Fiction Podcast* is a weekly show devoted to gay romance as well as pop culture. New episodes come out every Monday at BigGayFictionPodcast.com.

Learn more about Jeff, his books and find his social media links at JeffAdamsWrites.com.

www.ingramcontent.com/pod-product-compliance
Lightning Source LLC
Chambersburg PA
CBHW070517100726
47907CB00004B/871